THE
SILENT
STRIKER

PETE KALU

hope**road** : London

HopeRoad Publishing Ltd
P O Box 55544
Exhibition Road
London SW7 2DB

www.hoperoadpublishing.com

First Published by HopeRoad 2015

ISBN 978-1-908446-33-6

eISBN 978-1-908446-39-8

Printed and bound by
Lightning Source

Praise for The Silent Striker

'This is a book full to the brim with the joy, heartache and passion for the beautiful game. Along the way it deals with racism, disability, bullying, jealousy, young love, family life and friendship – all without a single patronising or forced word from beginning to end. It is written in beautiful clear prose and tells a story that every lover of football and life will instantly understand' **Melvin Burgess**

'YA novels featuring a protagonist from a "culturally diverse" space are rare. Pete Kalu's, *The Silent Striker* in which Marcus, a gifted footballer, confronts and overcomes many of the challenges of young people his age, is a welcome addition to British writing in this genre. *The Silent Striker* is a strong inspirational story about human aspiration, overcoming and achievement.' **Jacob Ross, author**

'Touching, funny and well tackled!' **Dr Muli Amaye, novelist**

'A richly compelling, emotionally resonant tale of courage.' **Melanie Amri, award-winning author**

'I have never understood the bigotry that has existed against deafness so I welcome a story that discusses it alongside cultural identity in a voice that is clear and understanding. This is a book that needs to be sat on every school library shelf as well as a role model of achievement. Well done Kalu.' **SuAndi, OBE**

'A compelling story about a boy losing his hearing. Pete Kalu is a wise and sensitive storyteller.' **Rajeev Balasubramanyam, author**

PETE KALU is a novelist, playwright and poet. His work has been widely published, performed and displayed within the UK. Prizes include a BBC Young Playwrights Award, the Liverpool /Kodak Film Pitch Award, *The Voice*/Jamaica Information Service Marcus Garvey Scholarship Award and Contact/BBC Dangerous Comedy Prize. He was elected a Fellow of the Royal Society of Arts in 2013. He is currently a PhD research student in Creative Writing at Lancaster University.

For Jakob, who placed his hand on my record player, showing me how music could be felt as well as heard. And for my brother, Jonah, whose footballing skills I always admired.

THE SEMI FINAL

Marcus looked around the field for someone to play the ball to. Nobody wanted it. He shimmied past two midfielders and fired a pass up to Horse. Horse tripped over his own feet. The ball rolled out for a throw-in. Marcus groaned. It was like everyone had put their boots on backwards.

At last, the referee blew his whistle. Half-time.

Marcus took in the panorama. That was what the art teacher had called it. Two tower blocks, a housing estate, a scrap cars yard, the supermarket slip road and Ducie High School 'A' Block. And rain.

'What are you looking at the sky for, Marcus? I said get over here!' yelled Mr Davies, the coach. Marcus jogged over to catch up with the rest of the team by the touchline. He sat on the soaking wet grass sucking on an orange slice as the coach laid into them good and proper.

'You numbing knuckleheads, we might as well all go home. This isn't double maths. Marcus, step it up. Horse, pass, move, look, call, positions! Rocket hug the touchline. Come on. Get past this Chorlton Academy rabble and we're in the final. It's there for the taking. Do you want it?'

'Yeah,' Marcus mumbled, along with the rest of the team. They lost the semi-final last year and the year before that. It felt like things were going the same way now. All the other Years had been knocked out of their Cup competitions.

'I didn't hear you,' yelled the coach, 'do you want it? Or should we all just give up and go home?'

There was silence.

'I'll arrange double rice pudding at the canteen for you all if we win,' said the coach. 'Can't get better than that, right? Dinners? Horse?'

Everyone laughed.

'Okay, that's the spirit. Come on lads, up you get. Marcus over here a minute.'

Marcus followed the coach, who, he decided, was built like an upside down street sweeping machine. The coach had a bin-like body and a head of bristle hair that stuck out sideways. And he went up and down in straight lines, making a lot of noise. He liked the coach. Mr Davies led him a little away from the rest of the team to where a tall, thin man was standing.

'Marcus, get the ball and do your thing, it's time to turn it on, right?' the coach said.

Marcus nodded. He looked briefly at the man standing next to the coach. He had the sharp, assessing look of a football scout. They always came to the big matches.

'I'm ready.'

'Go on then, start playing.'

Marcus trotted back towards the centre circle. When he turned round, the coach was deep in conversation. Marcus saw the coach mouth 'estate kids' and 'motivation'. He didn't catch the rest.

He made his way to his position in the centre of the midfield. The wind was coming at them sideways now, driving rain through their Ducie High jerseys.

At the restart, the Chorlton left-winger raced all the way to the touchline then crossed. Only a diving save from their keeper stopped Chorlton scoring.

On the touchline, Mr Davies did a puppet dance in his sleeping-bag-coat (a coat that looked like a sleeping bag), screaming at Dinners and then at Horse, telling them to give Marcus the ball.

Horse booted it to him. The ball dropped at Marcus's feet. Marcus looked up. The Chorlton goalkeeper was leaning on the post, picking his nose. After fifty minutes and not one shot even close to his goal, Marcus could see his point.

Somewhere inside his head he heard his dad singing a song, *I Who Have Nothing*. He loved that song. His dad was a balding Rasta who loved wailing this ballad by an afro-bobbed disco queen called Sylvester.

Something clicked in Marcus. He slipped the ball through to Rocket who trapped it, sprinted along the touchline then laid if off to Marcus again.

I Who Have Nothing was still playing in Marcus's head. It blanked out everything else except the rhythm of the game and in that moment the football became music.

Marcus danced the ball forward. His marker hesitated, dithering whether to close him down or zone him out wide to the wing.

Meanwhile, Horse was waving like mad, making for the near post, their keeper tracking him.

Their left-back is titchy, Marcus realised. He sped forward, looked up for one last check, then, as the defender's tackle smacked into him, he let the ball fly.

The ball looped up, the wind clawed it, flung it higher. The left-back leapt for all he was worth but the ball was already behind him. Their goalkeeper simply watched. Maybe there was an element of luck. The wind pushed it a metre further inside the upright than he'd intended.

1–0.

Mr Davies danced a jig. Marcus picked himself up and trotted back, taking high fives from Rocket and Horse. Briefly, he scanned the touchline for his dad, even though he knew his dad was on the early evening shift. He saw Leonard, the Ducie substitute, arms folded in the rain. He saw the thin man nodding. But Marcus's dad wasn't there.

'You okay?'

It was Horse. He was pointing to Marcus' left shin. There was a streak of blood where the defender's studs had caught him.

'Looks worse than it is,' Marcus said. 'Switch sides and I'll fly them over for you.'

The final. He was not going to let it go now. Marcus turned it on. From the kick-off they won the ball back from Chorlton and Horse got it to Marcus again. Marcus made a fool of his marker, dragged the ball back twice and span away from him. The Chorlton defence back-pedalled.

Marcus stopped and placed a foot on the ball. Still no Chorlton midfield player wanted to tackle him. The Chorlton coach was chopping the air on the other touchline.

Someone slid in on him. Marcus dinked the ball over the tackler's leg and vaulted forwards.

Ducie poured into the Chorlton penalty area. Marcus could pass to three different players. But he saw the goalkeeper was out of position. He rifled a shot straight into the top middle of the Chorlton net.

2–0.

It was a rout after that. The Chorlton players' heads dropped. They looked like they wanted the game over. Horse barged his way straight through the heart of the Chorlton defence and tapped it to Marcus who danced the ball into the net.

3–0.

Ducie ran out 4–0 winners and Marcus picked up man of the match from the referee. He got to keep the match ball. They made their way to the changing room in a carnival of studs and back-slapping and cheers. As everyone got changed, Mr Davies collared Marcus from the changing room. He pointed. The thin man was waiting to meet him in the coach's changing room office. They went over and Mr Davies introduced them:

'Marcus is our Messi, our Ronaldo. Marcus, this is Mr Peabody, a scout from Manchester United. He's looking to sign someone up as an apprentice.'

Another player popped his head round the coach's office door. 'Sir!' The coach dismissed him:

'Not now, Leonard. Go collect the water bottles.'

Leonard disappeared, but not before giving Marcus an ugly look.

'I'm not the main scout,' Mr Peabody said to Marcus, 'Nobody's sent me to Brazil or Italy yet.' The scout had a friendly face. He stretched out his hand to Marcus. 'Well played lad … on the whole.'

Marcus shook his hand. He had watched the thin man's lips so he knew he had said a word before 'on the whole' but he didn't know what that word was.

The coach gushed again at Mr Peabody. 'Marcus, he's so calm, in all the noise and fire, he can see an opportunity. He makes the right move every time, just glides in and "bam!" He's our silent striker.'

'Though sometimes he disappears, wouldn't you say?' Mr Peabody added, smiling again at Marcus to take the edge off the criticism.

'Yes,' the coach admitted. 'Starts staring at the sky or at his boots. I've told you that haven't I, Marcus? The best players stay focused.'

A Manchester United coach was here and interested in him. A Man United coach. This was amazing, Marcus thought. And they'd won. They had broken their semi-final jinx and they were in the final. Marcus bounced the match ball on the coach's office floor. This ATC now belonged to him. It was no ordinary ball. It was an Adidas Teamfeist Capitano. He was not going to let it out of his sight.

The coach had his arm around Marcus's shoulder and led him and the scout back into the changing room, then shouted out above the din:

'Well done, lads. Bit of hush please. This gentleman with me is a Manchester United agent.'

Jaws dropped in the changing room. Mr Peabody shuffled his feet, embarrassed.

'He liked what he saw. Particularly Marcus today. When Marcus gets going, he doesn't stop. That last goal, the whistle blew, you played the extra second after the whistle, didn't you, Marcus? Got the shot away, the referee allowed it. Technically, the ref's wrong there, but there's a message in that, isn't there, Mr Peabody? Stick the ball in the net and worry about all the rest after.'

'He bagged the goal,' Mr Peabody agreed. 'A different ref and he could have been sent off.'

Marcus thought quietly to himself that he hadn't heard the whistle, that was why he had played on, but he said nothing. It didn't matter now.

'Marcus bagged the goal,' repeated the coach. 'We're on our way to the final, boys. We can win it. Only Bowker Vale between us and glory. Each and every one of you, you've got training tomorrow evening, on the dot, no latecomers, no excuses.' The coach rubbed his hands. 'C'mon! We can win this!'

REFLECT QUIETLY ON THE ERROR OF YOUR WAYS (A.K.A. FRIDAY AFTERNOON DETENTION CLASS)

Mr Chips was running the afternoon detention class. Marcus knew the ropes. He chose a desk at the back and slumped in his chair. Another fifteen minutes of his life about to be wasted. There were eighteen of them in detention. It was a disused classroom in 'B' Block with a ripped out ceiling. Some people said it had had asbestos in it that could kill you. Others said it used to be a store room for canoes. It smelt of mould. Mr Chips got into his groove:

'Fold your arms, sit down, and be quiet. You are here for misbehaviour. Those of you who have been fighting, think of other ways you could have resolved your conflict. Without resorting to pushing people's heads into doors, Benjamin.'

Marcus settled back. He actually enjoyed Mr Chips's little roastings.

Mr Chips continued: 'Those of you who have been late to arrive at class, think about what steps you could take to get to class on time. Such as not stopping in the corridors to compare notes on boys you fancy. Kayleigh. Abigail. Those of you who have been misbehaving in class, consider the effect your behaviour has on others who want to learn, but can't because of you. Not everybody in class wants to indulge in a farting competition. Andrew. Mustapha. Those of you who are here for any other reason, reflect quietly on the error of your ways.' Mr Chips craned his eagle head. 'There will be no talking. Else you will be here again tomorrow. And you wouldn't want that, would you?'

'No, sir, I've got basketball practice at break tomorrow!' chirped some fool Year 7 boy Marcus did not know.

'Which part of "there will be no talking" did you not understand, Imtiaz?' shot Mr Chips.

'But you asked a question, Sir!'

'That question was rhetorical. Does anybody here know what "rhetorical" means? Look it up in your dictionaries.'

'I don't have a dictionary, Sir.'

Mr Chips sighed theatrically. 'A rhetorical question, Imtiaz, is one which does not require an answer. Now silence, while you all reflect. I want to hear only the sound of your brains humming with reflection.'

Life was basically unfair. That was Marcus's conclusion. He was sick of this school, sick of this detention class, sick of all his teachers, And totally sick of the geography teacher, Miss Podborsky. It had kicked off in geography. He had been sitting as usual at the back table when Jamil nudged him in the ribs. He looked up. Miss Podborsky was rolling her eyes at him.

'Marcus, do you have a medical condition that prevents you from folding your arms?'

The class laughed. Marcus felt humiliated. It was not as if he had been daydreaming. He had been working hard measuring the distance on the map from Field C to Field E.

'I'm sorry Miss, I didn't hear you.'

'You have very selective hearing, don't you, Marcus?'

Marcus didn't know what she meant but everybody laughed again.

Miss Podborsky seemed to have it in for him after that. The map exercises soon ended and she started going back over what they had learned this term:

'What is the name of the highest cloud?' Miss Podborsky asked. 'Don't call out. Let's have some fun. Whisper your answer to the person next to you and that person write your answer down, so you can't all change your answers, then we'll go round and see who has been paying attention this term.'

Marcus whispered 'cirrus' to Jamil. Jamil wrote that down then whispered something back to him. Marcus didn't catch it, but it didn't matter. He would just wait and see what Hannah, the cleverest girl in class thought it was, and give that as Jamil's answer. He was ready.

'Okay, pens down.' Miss Podborsky's inscrutable moon face with the slightly bloodshot eyes glanced around the room. She alighted on Hannah. She paused. Then carried on looking, swishing her eyes, left then right. She was a frustrated drama teacher, Marcus thought. 'Marcus, what was Jamil's answer?'

Miss had chosen him first. She'd never done that before, he was an expert in ducking teacher's questions. 'Er, I've forgotten, Miss.'

'What do you mean, "forgotten"?'

'I didn't write it down.'

Miss Podborsky let out a loud sigh. 'Jamil, whisper it to him again.'

Jamil whispered. It sounded like 'nummus' to Marcus. But that wasn't a cloud, he was sure. All eyes were on him.

'Cirrus,' Marcus said.

'Correct,' declared Miss Podborsky. 'Well done, Jamil.'

Jamil lapped up the praise then winked at Marcus.

The bell went.

'Okay, off you go,' Miss Podborsky said. 'Except Marcus, Marcus wait behind, please.'

Miss Podborsky kept him waiting in his seat while she did whatever teachers do with their lesson paperwork. Marcus looked around. His work from Year 7 had once hung on that wall to his left. Now some other Year 7 kid's work had taken his place. Nothing he had produced since then had been good enough to go up. Andrew's chart of the cycle of water had pride of place above the white board. Hannah's explanations of GPS positioning covered the peeling paint caused by a leak from a drainage pipe carrying toilet waste. The room had been nicknamed 'The Stinker' after that leak, and nobody who sat there ever sat comfortably again.

Miss Podborsky approached him. She told him off in a tumble of words he could hardly keep up with. His hearing always got worse under stress, he knew. They thought he was cheeky if he stared at them, yet if he looked away, he didn't hear them as well. Why was that?

'You need to take … smirk off your face, do you wish to know … you are sat here? You are a disruptive … in the class, what happened to… Marcus of last year? You … not have helped Jamil who obviously did not … the

11

answer. You have an attitude, Marcus and if you … shape up soon, I will be placing you on report!'

'But Miss I wasn't ignoring you,' Marcus protested. 'I was concentrating on my work. And Jamil—'

But Miss Podborsky was having none of it. 'You are a bright boy, Marcus and I will not allow you to waste your talent. For now, I am merely placing you in afternoon detention. But be warned. I have my eyes on you. And I will not allow my lessons to be disrupted. Not at all.'

Fine, Marcus thought. She did not want him to waste his talent, so she was putting him in detention. Where he would sit, doing nothing, wasting his talent. And he had done nothing wrong anyway. School sucked. There was no justice in the world.

'Marcus Adenuga, are you reflecting on the error of your ways?' boomed Mr Chips, suddenly right next to him.

He had been, Marcus thought, until Mr Chips had disturbed him. 'Yes Sir.'

'And have you gained any insight by that reflection?'

'Yes Sir.'

'And would you like to share that insight with us?'

Everyone was looking at him. Marcus imagined even the mould spores that had to be circling in the damp detention room air had stopped and were waiting for his answer.

'No Sir,' he said.

Mr Chips' brow plunged, his hawk eyes zoomed down on Marcus. Then a miracle happened, he relented, and moved on to torment someone else in detention class:

'Is someone humming? Humming, whistling, singing and all variations on the acoustic spectrum is not silence!'

Marcus's mind wandered to his dad's singing. He could still remember calling out, 'That's my Daddy!' when his dad had taken to the stage of some pub in a silver suit and burst into *Blue Suede Shoes*. He'd been 'Tony the Black Elvis' back then. Marcus must have been about four, he thought. It was a time B. T. S: Before The Sister. Leah was a complete nuisance, even though he couldn't imagine life without her now. When she cried at night Mum sometimes put her in his bed and then she'd wriggle and crawl and he never got to sleep till late and was dog-tired the next day, didn't pay attention in class and ended up in here, in detention, watching imaginary spores floating in the air.

Mr Chips finally called an end to their boredom. 'You may leave the room. Single file please, starting from the front.'

There was a mass scraping of chairs and everyone rushed for the door. Fifteen minutes of my life wasted, Marcus muttered to himself. Fifteen minutes of football practice thrown away. It was plain stupidity. School sucked.

FRIDAY AGAIN

Friday was Marcus's least favourite day and geography was his least favourite lesson. He trooped in to the classroom along with everyone else and sat down at his desk and the class quickly settled down to study. Jamil was soon sleeping. He was like those batteries that gave off mega-watts until they suddenly and completely expired. Late afternoon, no matter how many energy drinks he'd had for lunch, Jamil would be found with his arms over his head, sleeping in class, especially on a Friday. Marcus could do with a snooze himself. In the morning he'd had to feed Leah instead of ironing his uniform. Leah had flicked the egg yolk at him and he was sure there was still some in his hair. He moved his compass around the exercise paper. The teacher occasionally looked across at him, but mainly, she was marking. Horse sat in front of Marcus and Marcus shifted to hide himself from the teacher behind Horse's frame. Horse smiled without looking up, knowing what he was doing. Horse had a big back, broad legs and feet that turned outwards. When he walked he owned the pavement, he bowled along. He had skin the colour of sunflower seeds, short eyebrows and steady, almond eyes that were warm and unafraid and somehow saw deep into people. Marcus nudged Jamil awake; Miss was looking over at them again. Things went okay and Marcus kept his head down, but towards the end of the lesson Miss Podborsky picked him out.

'Marcus Adenuga you've been very quiet today. Come to the front of the classroom.'

Marcus shoved his chair back and dragged himself to the front of the class. Everybody had stopped work to watch. Nobody had been called out to the front of class by Miss Podborsky before.

'Let's see how much you have learned so far, Marcus. Explain to the class the meaning of precipitation. Big loud voice, please.'

'I was off ill that week,' Marcus said.

'Excuses. You've had plenty of time to catch up. Come on.'

Miss Podborsky circled him as she waited. 'Look at you, Marcus. Odd socks. Trousers … crumpled.'

Marcus held his breath. He hardly heard Miss Podborsky anymore; he just concentrated on remaining calm during the shaming.

'Have you … brought up or dragged up? And don't tell me your family can't afford an iron. As the clothes, so the boy. Precipitation. Meaning. Please.'

Marcus went to open his mouth but no words were supplied to his tongue by his brain.

'Well? We are waiting,' said Miss Podborsky.

'Water in the air, Miss?' Marcus managed.

'"Water in the air". How very precise,' Miss Podborsky mocked. The class all tittered. 'You will have to do better than that if you want to sit down again.'

Miss Podborsky was standing beside him, mocking the way he was biting his lower lip. She said, 'I'll give you a clue. Falling water.'

Marcus thought. Still nothing came to his mind. Miss Podborsky issued another 'Well?'

One of the girls put her hand up. 'Please Miss, he's crying, Miss.'

Marcus felt his face. There were wet streaks on his cheeks.

The class went quiet.

'Go and sit down, Marcus,' Miss Podborsky said quickly. 'And concentrate better next time. French children are so much better behaved.'

'Fuck you,' Marcus thought, as he walked back to his seat. His whole face had heated up.

'What did you say?' Miss Podborsky shouted across to him.

So he hadn't just thought it, Marcus realised. He had actually said it.

'Nothing,' he replied to Miss Podborsky. He didn't care anymore, he just wanted to get away. Every second spent in this class was a waste of his life.

Afterwards, nobody mentioned what happened. Marcus splashed water on his face in the toilets then leaned on a radiator and stared out of the toilet window at the clouds. Friday was football training. At least there was that.

Training went well. He liked the shooting exercises, the dribbling and the fitness drills. Running around lifted his spirits. They did an hour then the coach and most of the squad drifted back to the changing room.

Horse stayed behind with Marcus on the field so he could work on a new move he'd been trying. It was called the 'Cruyff Turn'. He had been practicing it on the pitch, if you could describe the small patch of tarmac in the park near his house as a pitch. Every morning for a week he had tried the move without success. Horse gamely ran at him like a defender while Marcus twisted one way but turned the other with the ball.

'You okay? You must hate Podborsky,' Horse said.

'I'm fine, let's keep at this. Close me down faster.'

Horse ran at him again and again. After two hours, Marcus finally nailed it. Horse slapped him on the back. 'Massive, Marky, like a magician!'

'Thanks, but it's still not right.'

Marcus insisted they did it a few more times. By then it was pitch dark. They ran back to the changing room. When they were finally back in their uniforms, Marcus checked his phone and saw his mum had left five messages. The last one said she was about to call the police. He had no credit on his phone, neither had Horse. They ran home together, splitting when they reached the housing estate.

He let himself in. His mum ranted and raved as he ate his dinner in the living room with the TV turned down low.

'I almost called the police!' she said, whacking a spoonful of jollof rice onto his plate. 'And now I have to see the Head.' She headed back into the kitchen.

'What?' said Marcus, shocked.

She came back out with a piece of chicken. 'The Head rang, left a message. I have to go see her, with you, first thing, Monday.'

'They only call parents in if they're expelling someone,' Marcus said.

That really set his mum off. 'What the blazes have you been up to at school?' She chucked a chicken piece onto his plate with a spoon.

'I— ' began Marcus.

'Don't bother telling me. Getting expelled, that's what! Eat your tea and go straight to bed. As if I don't have enough problems! A sick baby. My asthma flaring. A witless husband. And now this!' His mum stormed back into the kitchen, slamming the door behind her.

It had to be Miss Podborsky, Marcus decided. If he had a voodoo doll he'd imagine it was Miss Podborsky then stick pins in it till it was a mass of broken threads. Marcus hated her so much he noticed he clenched his teeth whenever he thought of her. He held onto his ATC ball under his pillow. At least the football training had gone well. The Cryuff Turn. It was all in the hips. He still didn't think he was doing it as well as Cryuff himself. He'd seen the Cryuff videos on YouTube.

The next morning Marcus got out of bed early and made himself some sandwiches. He stayed out all day on the pitch, practising. When he played football he forgot all about his troubles. The longer he played, the more he forgot. At lunchtime he bought chips and gravy from the chippy, then went back to the pitch and played on. He texted his mum to let her know where he was, so she wouldn't call the police. Only when it got so dark he couldn't see the goal wall, did he go back home. He kicked off his shoes at the door. Leah's buggy wasn't in the room so Dad must have taken her out. He called out. 'Mum, I'm home, what's to eat?'

His mum appeared at the kitchen door with a measuring tape in one hand and a pencil in her other. She stared at him and sighed. 'Marcus, the greatest magic I ever did was making you.'

What had got into his mum? Marcus thought. Yesterday she had been shouting at him, now she was like this. Even though he knew there was nobody else in the room, he looked around. 'Hush, Mum, you're embarrassing me.'

'I don't care. You can grow as many moustache hairs as you like, you'll always be my baby. The most beautiful boy in the world and I pushed him out into the world.'

'Mum.'

'I love my son! Did everybody hear that? I love my son!' his mum shouted at the top of her voice.

'Right. Tell the whole street.'

As he brushed passed her into the kitchen she tickled him in the ribs till he laughed. His mum was always happier at weekends. Maybe she felt bad about shouting at him so much yesterday.

Monday morning came round and Marcus sat with his mum in the taxi to school. Mum's mood was not good and neither was his own. He thought about what had happened. Yes, he shouldn't have sworn at Miss Podborsky and yes, he had not handed in two of her homework assignments. Still, there was no way he had been so bad that he had to be expelled. When they caught that boy on the playground CCTV scratching up the history teacher's car, he hadn't been expelled. When Leonard had slammed the art tutor's door so hard an oil painting had fallen off the wall and shattered, he was only placed on report. When two Year 10 girls had fought at dinner break and one had ended up with a black eye and the other with a clump of hair missing from the back of her head, they had been placed in isolation for one week, nothing more. So why was he the one to be expelled?

They entered the school building and school administrator showed them along a corridor to the

Head's office. The administrator said that the Head would not be long and to sit on the chairs outside.

Marcus watched his mum drumming on her chair with her fingers. Rap-a-tap. Rap-a-tap. Rap. Her breathing was wheezy again. She was trying to smile confidently but every so often she shot him an angry glance. She had hardly spoken to him in the taxi. Leah had puked a little on her work blouse. His mum had dabbed the puke off but the stain still showed in a hexagonal patch.

The Head appeared from behind her door. Ropey Face was all smiles. The happy executioner. 'Mrs Adenuga? Marcus? Come in please.'

Marcus walked in behind his mum, dragging his feet. Mr Wrexham, the head of year was in the room too. Ropey Face and Ozone together. This was serious. Marcus wondered if Burnage Academy would have him. But which school took rejects from Ducie High?

Everyone sat down. The Head offered a glass of water to his mum, which she declined.

'Shall we begin?' said the Head. 'By all reports Marcus is a very bright pupil, but we have had some concern about his progress this term.'

Here we go, thought Marcus.

'I've told him to sort himself out,' his mum said quickly, 'if he doesn't knuckle down, he'll be grounded for a month and he's on hoovering duty and making up the baby food as well, as extra punishment.'

'Thanks, Mum,' said Marcus, to himself.

'I'm glad you share our concerns, Mrs Adenuga', said Ropey Face.

'He's very sorry. I've never known him so sorry. You're so sorry, aren't you, Marcus?'

Marcus nodded and did his sorry face. In these circumstances his mum was a force of nature not to be messed with.

'Give him another chance, please, before you expel him.'

The Head looked surprised. 'Expel him? He's one of our most promising pupils. Nothing could be further from our thoughts.'

Marcus's mum looked to Marcus. Marcus looked back at her, as puzzled as she was.

Ozone weighed in. 'His maths results are exceptional. Maybe there has been some confusion. This is not about expulsion, Mrs Adenuga, this meeting is about helping Marcus.'

Ozone was looking at Marcus encouragingly, shaking his spiky hair in a happy clappy way. Marcus was not convinced.

Ropey Face continued. 'Mrs Adenuga, we have a system in place that allows us to monitor pupils' behaviour in all their classes.' She tapped a computer print-out. 'It's a new system from France. It tries to notice patterns and spot problems that may not be apparent to any one class teacher. We're the only school in our area that has this.'

'Isn't that fantastic, Marcus?' said Marcus's mum. Marcus could tell from her voice she had no idea what the Head was talking about.

'It was introduced by our Head of Innovation, Mrs Podborsky.' The Head's chin rose with pride. 'And what this system is telling us,' said the Head, patting the pile of printouts on her desk, 'is that Marcus may have a slight problem with his hearing.'

Marcus frowned. This was rubbish. Typical Miss Podborsky, messing with him.

'Okay, carry on,' said his mum, suddenly upbeat. 'He was at the doctors only recently with flu and they checked his ears for wax then. But that's what this … system says?'

Marcus listened to his mum, suddenly talking to the Head as though she was close to completing a deal to sell the Head some double-glazing. It made Marcus laugh silently.

'Yes, and we would like to propose a couple of things as suggested by the software.' She patted the print-out again. 'Firstly, if he's already been checked for wax, then we'd want to book him an appointment for a hearing test at the local clinic. It's a simple thing to arrange if you consent.'

'By all means, I'm sure it's a waste of …' his mum said, but did not finish.

Ropey Face's phone was ringing. Ozone picked it up, spoke briefly then put it back down.

'And in the meantime,' the Head resumed, 'we'd like to have Marcus sit closer to his teachers, at the front of the class instead of at the back where he usually is.' Ropey Face smiled at Marcus at this point. Marcus smiled back through tight lips. The Head spoke to him directly for the first time: 'You do understand, Marcus, moving you towards the front of the class is not a punishment. It's a temporary measure that may help you until you have had your ears checked. It's just a precaution.'

'So I can move back afterwards?'

'Yes, of course,' said the Head, 'once we have eliminated this as a possibility. That's a promise.'

The Head's phone was ringing again. 'Are we all agreed then?' she smiled.

Marcus's mum nodded. The Head looked at him. Marcus nodded too.

'Okay Marcus, we will inform the teachers and make the arrangements.' She stood up and shook Marcus's mum's hand. Ozone ushered them out.

'All that over a bit of wax,' laughed his mum when they were outside on the street.

Marcus felt relieved and troubled at the same time. He dreaded having to sit at the front of class. It was where all the goody two-shoes sat. And he didn't want to be split up from Jamil either. They sat together in class always, and Jamil never sat at the front, he needed his sleep too much.

TWO STORMS AND A HAT TRICK

The day after the meeting with the Head, Marcus gobbled up his beans on toast and headed for school. His mum had calmed down and gave him a hug before he set off. There was just this nonsense about where he was going to be sitting at school to get through.

At the bus stop, he did keepy-uppy with his ATC. A small crowd watched him. He didn't mind. The thing was, it was his last chance to practice before two hours of lessons. Some kid tried to take the ball off him but he dribbled around him four times till the kid sat down and crossed his legs, defeated. Marcus switched to headers. He rattled off thirty-six on the trot when the crowd started pointing and shouting. He nestled the ball between his shoulders and looked. A big black 4 by 4 with tinted windows had pulled over. Marcus recognised it. It went past most mornings. The passenger window had rolled down and someone was leaning out. 'Marcus … if …?' they shouted. He didn't catch the '…' but he thought he recognised the figure in the passenger seat. He flicked the ball into his hands and walked to the car. 'Hi Anthony, wassup?'

Anthony was the captain of Bowker Vale. Last year Bowker had done the double: won the league and Cup. He'd met Anthony at the Gifted & Talented Summer Football School soon after. The first day of summer school, he'd been paired with him. They had got on fine, but when lunchtime arrived, Marcus realised he had forgotten to bring his sandwiches and drink. Anthony had refused to share his own sandwiches with him and instead pointed him to the vending machine even though he knew Marcus had no money. Marcus had shrugged it off.

'It's all good,' Anthony replied, a toothy smile on his face. Marcus nodded to Anthony's dad at the driving wheel. He had a sunbed tan and a Beckham haircut. He was wearing a pinstripe suit. It was the first time Marcus had seen someone wearing one in person and not on TV. He looked like a big boss.

'Get in, we'll drop you at your school,' Anthony said.

Marcus hesitated.

The back door thunked open. There was someone in the back already.

'That's my sister,' said Anthony. 'She's a pain in the arse but you'll have to put up with her.'

His sister pulled a face at her brother. 'I'm Adele,' she said to Marcus, 'please ignore my feckless brother.' She patted the seat beside her for him to sit.

Marcus climbed in, buckled up and the car got moving. 'How's it going Marcus?' said Anthony's dad.

'Good, good,' Marcus replied warily.

'I heard you played a blinder in your match last week,' his dad said, 'out of this world.'

'We did okay.'

'4–0, and you got three, that's more than okay. They said you were Houdini!'

'Who's he play for?' Marcus asked Anthony's dad politely.

'Like nobody could get near you,' Anthony explained.

Marcus shrugged. 'If they give us the space, we'll play. That's what the point of the diamond does. That's my game.'

'Out of this world you played, apparently,' repeated Marcus's dad.

Marcus felt awkward. Finally he said, 'you were "Most Valuable Player" last year in the league, weren't you, Anthony?'

'Yeh,' said Anthony proudly, then, 'the scouts are all watching me now.'

'He could learn a thing or two from you though,' his dad said to Marcus. 'How you were keeping the ball up back there.'

Marcus shrugged. 'Our coach says it's circus stuff.'

'No, it's good,' said Anthony, 'gets you out of tight spots, like being man marked. It's good if you can control your headers, your chest cushions, your knee pull-downs, all your balls like that. The scouts like it.'

Adele snorted.

'What's wrong with Adele?' their dad asked.

'Can you "control all your balls" like that, Anthony?' Adele said, giggling away.

'Adele, raise the tone!' said their dad. 'What's got into you?'

'So, Marcus, how does it feel to know people are envious of your talent?' said Adele, unfazed.

'I'm not envious,' snapped Anthony. 'I've got my game, he's got his.'

'You are! You just said back there, "I wish I had the skills like him", that's why we pulled over.'

'Adele!' their dad interrupted.

Marcus didn't like this piggy-in-the-middle feeling he was getting. 'Anthony plays a different game to me,' he explained to Adele, turning to look at her. As he looked, she cocked her head towards him, disarming him completely. She put her hand on his.

'You were saying?' she asked.

Suddenly Marcus was confused. His body flushed. He couldn't take his eyes off her. 'What I mean is, if we were ever in a team together, we'd be the …'

'The what?' Adele asked, moving her head even closer to his.

'The dream team,' Anthony finished for him. 'Put it there!'

Anthony had turned and he and Marcus high-fived. He leaned back, glanced at Adele again and wondered how he could find himself fancying her even though he'd known her for only one minute. He sneaked a look at her. She was sneaking a look at him at exactly the same moment. They did a double take and she smiled. He shook his head, embarrassed, happy and confused at the same time. This was complicated. Trust Anthony to have a gorgeous sister.

The car purred on. It was air conditioned, with high leather seats, tinted windows and holders for mobile phones and cups. Anthony and his dad began talking about repairing a fence.

Adele nudged him. 'Have you got your phone?'

'Yep,' said Marcus.

'Bring your number up.'

He did.

Adele copied his number into her own phone. She dialled him and his phone lit up. 'Nice,' she said. Then she texted him:

Phne me 2nite f u dare!

He smiled at her and nodded. What was her game? He couldn't date his rival's sister. No way. As if replying to his thought, she pulled a funny face, her lower lip going one way, her upper lip the other and everything looking squashed in between. You had to smile. She was nuts, Marcus concluded.

The car pulled up. 'Here you go, Marcus, have a top day at school.'

'Thanks Mr …'

'Vialli,' Anthony's dad said.

'Thanks Mr Vialli.'

'Any time.'

'See ya!' called out Anthony as Marcus bundled himself, his ATC and his school bag out of the car.

'See ya!' Adele called, mimicking her brother.

Marcus waved them off. Then he juggled his ball, left foot, right foot, all the way to the school gates, thinking about Adele.

At school, maths was okay. He and Jamil were moved together to a table closer to the front but not the actual front. They sat with Dinners and Zahra. Though Dinners was large, he could do the shuffle and girls were always laughing at his jokes. He was famous for burning his eyelashes off in a science experiment in Year 7. Sometimes he still plucked at his eyelashes. Dinners spent the maths class discussing mascara with Zahra in between both of them asking Marcus to help them with their geometry. The way Zahra twisted her hair when she was doing her work made him think of Adele. Adele's skin was a light brown. Italian, he guessed, almost the same colour as Zahra's.

In English, the tables were laid out in a horseshoe shape, so he was moved three seats closer to where the teacher most often stood, and he noticed the teacher spent more time standing close to him when she talked to the class than she usually did.

On Friday, Marcus braced himself – there was geography to get through and he groaned inwardly. He'd thought about staying off ill, but with the mood his mum was in, that was impossible. Besides, there was the league match after school: he couldn't phone in ill for geography, then turn up for the match claiming a miraculous recovery.

Outside the classroom, Marcus stood in line. He smoothed his clothes. He'd made sure he'd ironed them this morning. His socks matched. He wondered about Miss Podborsky. Was she messing with him by sending him for the hearing test? Or did she really care, as his mum suggested, and he just needed to make more effort with her? They went in. Miss Podborsky insisted he sit at the desk to her left, the one underneath the dodgy wastepipe. Jamil asked if he could sit there too, and she let him. Every five minutes Miss Podborsky looked at Marcus the way Marcus imagined a spider looked at a fly that had landed in its web. They seemed to be spending forever on clouds and rain. Surely there was more to geography than water?

Late into the lesson, Miss Podborsky got up and wiggled her nose in the air. 'There's a strange smell in here,' she pronounced. She went round, sniffing the air every three steps. Finally she stopped right next to Marcus. She looked up. 'The pipe is def … tely not leaking today.' She bent low and sniffed Marcus's jacket.

'Marcus?'

'Yes, Miss?'

'Are you gonna make him stand up again, Miss?' shouted someone.

'No,' Miss Podborsky replied, 'not after last week's performance.'

Marcus bit his lower lip and felt the blood trickle along the insides of his mouth.

'But Marcus, what *is* that smell on you?'

She was pointing to his jacket lapels. Marcus looked at his jacket and saw the milky white patch.

'It's baby milk, Miss. I had to feed the baby this morning then burp her. She's got projectile vomiting.'

Miss Podborsky snorted. She looked him up and down then added: 'And I suppose you're also going to tell me the baby hid your pressing iron too!'

'But I ironed my clothes this morning, Miss, honest!'

'Well, I'm sure your mother didn't!'

The whole class screamed with laughter.

Marcus had had enough. What was it with this teacher? Even as Miss Podborsky tried to restore order, he stood up, packed his books into his bag and walked out.

Miss Podborsky shouted after him. 'Marcus, return here! You'll regret this!'

Marcus didn't regret it. At least he had controlled his tear ducts this time.

Miss Podborsky came running after him. Without her audience, she wasn't so scary. He stopped for her.

'I'm sorry, Marcus. I was out of order. Sometimes I say very daft things. I apologise. In France, we teach differently. But you have to return to the classroom. You're a bright pupil, you can do well.'

Marcus shook his head because he knew if he tried to talk he might cry. What he wanted to say was: Why do you humiliate me like this?

'Did the Head tell you about the possible hearing issue?'

Marcus nodded.

'I looked it up. I thought it might help. Me and you have just got off on the wrong foot, haven't we? Now come back into class and I won't report it.'

Why couldn't she be nice like this in class? Marcus thought. Adults were weird. He didn't trust her. He had had enough. He didn't care anymore. 'Report it. See if I care,' Marcus said. He swung away from her and down the corridor.

Marcus waited outside the changing room building, even though he knew the CCTV would be picking him up standing there during class hours, and questions would be asked. The match after school was an important game. They were running neck and neck with Bowker Vale in the league.

When school ended and everyone spilled out, Marcus was first into the changing room. He didn't check the team sheet. He knew he always played.

Mr Davies approached him. 'I heard something kicked off in your geography class today,' he said. 'Put it out of your mind, Marcus. Just think football, yeh?'

'Mr Davies?' someone said brightly. Marcus looked up. It was Leonard the substitute again. Leonard's face was always well oiled, like a ripe conker, fresh out of its shell. And he had perfect teeth. Everything about him was perfect. He had a confident smile and a dimple in his chin that somehow meant you couldn't help agree with him. Everybody agreed with Leonard. Except the coach. This wound Leonard up no end.

'What, Leonard? I'm talking to Marcus at the moment,' said the coach.

'Am I the substitute again, Sir?'

'Yes, Lenny. Now go fill the water bottles, good lad.'

Leonard clattered off to find the bottles without even a 'hi' to Marcus. Mr Davies carried on with his little pep talk to Marcus.

'So, Marcus, key word is focus, yes?'

'Okay.'

'Off you go then.'

When they made it onto the pitch, the head of year, Ozone, was talking with Mr Davies on the touchline. Leonard was doing a few ball tricks in front of them both but they paid no attention to him, they were deep in conversation. Both teachers glanced at Marcus and Mr Davies actually pointed at him once. Ozone's head was doing that Bollywood, yes–but–no shake to whatever Mr Davies was saying. Mr Davies was doing a lot of jabbing. Eventually the coach waved Marcus over.

'Like I said,' said Mr Davies, putting an arm around Marcus, 'he's absolutely blinding on the pitch. Trains harder than any other boy on the team. He's the jewel in the crown. The … pin. And he loves his football, don't you, Marcus?'

'Yes,' said Marcus warily. Why was Ozone here at all? He'd never shown an interest in the team before.

Mr Davies hadn't finished: 'Marcus, if there is one area of school life where you would say you were at your best, behaviour, performance, discipline, self-control, appetite wise, what would it be?'

'Dinner time,' said Marcus.

'Besides that, you ninny,' said Mr Davies.

'Football.'

'See? While he's got his football he's got something to play for, we see the best Marcus can be. Okay, Marcus, off you trot; referee's blowing for the kick-off.'

Somehow, Marcus knew the conversation had something to do with Miss Podborsky. And that it meant trouble. From the kick off, he played like he was on fire. All his anger about what had happened in Miss Podborsky's class came out on the pitch. He demanded the ball from Ira. He pushed Rocket further up the wing. He pulled Horse from left midfield to right. He ordered Jamil to run harder and faster across the goal mouth when he, Marcus, had the ball. Nobody argued with Marcus, not even the coach, not when he was in this mood.

A decent ball came to him out of defence. Marcus ran through the opponent's midfield like a bowling ball through skittles. He played a quick one-two with Jamil and raced towards goal.

That song, *I Who Have Nothing*, began playing once more in his head. When the ball dropped to him again on the edge of the area, he did his Cryuff Turn. He pulled it off perfectly. The two confused defenders ran into each other and fell at his feet. Marcus dragged the ball past them then chipped the goalkeeper. The net billowed. Horse whooped. 1–0.

Marcus looked to see where Ozone was. He was nowhere.

After his Cryuff Turn move, no defender went anywhere near Marcus for fear of being made to look a fool. Ducie surged forward again. A defender barged Jamil off the ball, just outside the penalty area. Jamil fell, grabbed the ball and turned to the referee. It was a free kick, within shooting distance. Marcus stepped up. If this went in, the match was as good as over. He eyed the goal and estimated the distance. The defending team had thrown up a wall of four players. Marcus strolled back three strides, and at the referee's signal, whipped a bending kick round the defensive wall. It curved smartly into the top right of the net. 2–0.

He scored his third with a looping header from a corner. It wasn't even half-time.

Ducie finished 6–1 winners. It was Marcus's second hat-trick of the season. Jamil, Horse, Rocket and the whole team sang his name all the way to the changing room.

In the changing room, the coach pulled Marcus to one side. 'Listen to me, Marcus, look at me. Right. I've never said this to any boy before and I even taught at Bowker Vale for a year, but here it is: I've never met a better player. You may be a council estate kid, but you are England material, understand? You could play for England.'

'Okay,' said Marcus, blushing. 'Thanks, Sir.'

Everybody must have overheard because a cheer went up in the changing room. 'Marcus for England! Marcus for England!' Somebody grabbed him and before he knew it, Marcus found himself on Horse's shoulders, ducking his head to avoid hitting the ceiling beams as Horse danced around the changing room with him on his shoulders to more shouts of 'Marcus for England!'

Marcus loved it.

Amid all the celebration he caught the look on Leonard's face. Leonard had not been brought on as a substitute at all, even when they had been 5–0 up. Everyone's face was ecstatic, except Leonard's who looked like he'd been chewing a lemon. Marcus felt sorry for him.

The coach dampened things down. 'That's enough lads, put him down. We don't want it going to his head!'

That night, Marcus kissed the ball and placed it back under the pillow. The beautiful game. Everything else in his mind disappeared when he thought football. All that stuff with Miss Podborsky vanished. He replayed in his mind each of his three goals. He couldn't sleep, he was too happy. The streetlight outside his bedroom window continued to flicker. The way the light flickered was exactly like a step-over move: On-Off. On-Off. On-Off. Gone. Step-over. Step-over. Step-over. Gone. He turned in his bed, still restless. He couldn't remember ever not playing football. He'd always kicked everything – tennis balls, drinks cans, crushed up sheets of paper, crisp bags, toilet rolls, rolled up gloves. His fifth birthday party had been a kick-about out on the pitch. At seven, he'd tried eating his dinner standing up in the backyard balancing the ball on a foot. For the last two years, every Saturday, he put in an hour's training on the pitch, way before any of his friends got up. It didn't matter if it was snow, rain, his birthday, if his mate had the latest PlayStation game, if his hair needed cutting. It all had to wait until after he'd practised. He slept with the ball, kissed it good night. It sat next to him at the dinner table. It was the first thing packed into his school bag.

At first, when he'd started the daily practice sessions, the ball was his fiercest enemy, fighting everything he tried to get it to do, bucking like a Doberman straining on a leash. Yet he kept at it. And slowly, the ball became his friend. He coaxed, cajoled, and soothed it. The ball learned to be calm with him and he'd send it exactly where it was needed. The ball trusted him.

Then one day something bizarre happened. People started to watch him practice. He remembered the first time. He'd gone to London with his mum for a funeral. That morning hadn't started well. Marcus had come down dressed and ready to go and plonked himself on the sofa next to his mum. His mum was dressed but she was sitting with a tissue in her hand, dabbing her eyes, a folder on her lap.

'Mum, what are you doing?'

'Going through old photos of you.'

'Why?'

'It's what mums do in films when they're sad, I thought I'd try it.'

'Does it work?'

'Yes.' His mum turned to him and cupped his face with her hand. 'Do you know what it is to love someone so much it hurts? That's how I feel about you every day Marcus, I want you to know that.'

'I love you too, Mum.'

His mum closed the folder and shuffled up. 'Remember to polish your shoes before you get out of the funeral car.'

'Yeah, whatever.'

That day they had driven down south then switched into the black car for the ride to the cemetery, where they found there was some delay, no-one knew why. Everybody stood about, not knowing what to do. Mum went off talking to other mourners. Marcus thought he'd try out a few moves in the cemetery car park. He didn't like funerals and practicing kept his mind off what was going on, namely a dead body being laid to rot in the ground. Marcus popped his ball out of his bag, trapped it, bounced it ten times on his head, then cushioned it onto his forehead, rolled it back between his shoulder blades, flipped it up, trapped it on one foot and held it there for ten, then flipped it up and juggled it in a sequence: left knee, left shoulder, head, right shoulder, right knee, right foot, nestle, cradle swap to left foot, then that sequence all over again. All the while eating from a bag of cheese-and-onion crisps.

Some boys from another funeral gathered round him. Their funeral had been delayed as well and there was nothing else to do. It was summer. They were wowed by his skills. When Marcus finally sat down with them on the bubbling car park tarmac, sweat poured off his brow, and his white shirt stuck to him like a wet flag of Brazil.

'C'mon, what's your secret?' they asked him. 'How did yer do that?'

Marcus shrugged and said in his best London twang. 'Just practice, innit? 24 7 12. Practice. Practice. Practice.'

'So that's all it is?' someone asked.

Marcus shrugged. 'Yeah, like. Practice, you know, practice, practice, practice.'

Then the funeral was back on. Everyone lined up by the big hole with the mound of earth behind it. Marcus's mum gave him a whack, for standing at the coffin with his ball in his hand. The ball dropped out of his hands. It bounced off the mound of earth and into the hole that had been dug for the coffin. Marcus tried to scramble down to get it out again, it was his favourite ball. Mum fainted. Everyone tugged Marcus back. The wailing got worse. The priest chanted above it all and the box got lowered. Now Marcus's Uncle Simon was buried with what had been Marcus's favourite ball underneath him.

Even now, even though he had his ATC, a part of Marcus resented that. Why hadn't they let him get it? What did his dead Uncle need his ball for? Sometimes he felt like going back down to that London graveyard and digging it out from under him.

Marcus shifted in his bed. A smile crept onto his face, as he remembered the match again. When it came to football, Marcus was good. Here, in his bed, there was no need for him to be humble about it. Now they were first in the league table, with Bowker Vale two points behind them. For the first time ever, Ducie looked set to win the league. Marcus reached out an arm and brought his ATC close so it pressed into his cheek. He fell asleep practicing Cryuff Turns in his head.

SPICY ABDUL'S CAPPUCCINO BURGER CAFE BAR

It was Saturday. Marcus looked at his tiny 'Single Party Cheeseburger' and his gloopy 'Mango Heaven Milkshake' and sighed. Adele was late. His legs were caked with mud from football. He'd raced off without showering so he could be here on time. He followed a fly that danced around from the display board to the motionless kebab spit before it keeled over and dropped into the fat catcher below the spit.

Adele had texted him saying they had to meet up because she needed to tell him something important. He had agreed out of boredom more than anything, he'd convinced himself, though that did not explain why his heart was racing.

The owner (presumably his name was Abdul, Marcus thought, though he had blonde hair and looked more like a Dave) was standing over him with a 'would-you-like-to-order-anything-else-sir' look. There were no other customers so what did it matter if he was sat here? He smiled a 'no thanks' to Abdul. Abdul sloped off.

When Adele arrived she had two big brown shopping bags and a bundle of excuses.

'It took me two buses to get here,' she said, collapsing into the chair next to him.

'What do you want to order?' said Abdul, from the till.

'A frothy-soya-mocha-with-cream top with chocolate sprinkles and vanilla syrup!' Adele said, like a film star.

'I'm not sure they do that here,' Marcus whispered.

'One frothy-soya-mocha-cream-top-chocolate sprinkles-vanilla syrup coming up!' said Abdul.

Abdul served the fancy coffee to Adele and went back to his stool by the till.

Adele sipped the coffee froth.

'What school do you go to?' Marcus asked. It was the only thing he could think of saying.

'St Elizabeth's.'

'Wow,' said Marcus. St Elizabeth's was the poshest school in the area.

'My Talented Brother goes to an even posher one. Bowker Vale,' Adele added.

'I know. "My Talented Brother". Is that your name for Anthony?'

'Yes. MTB for short. According to the whole world, MTB is *good-at-everything*. And I am *such-a-disappointment*.'

Marcus smiled. 'I bet you have some talent.'

'Shoplifting.' Adele reached inside her shopping bag and pulled out a silver necklace on a pad. 'Do you like this style? You can have it if you want.'

Marcus looked at the necklace. It was on a proper display pad. They didn't normally give buyers the pad when they bought things. Did they?

'No thanks. It's a girl's,' Marcus said.

'Oops. So what have you been up to?' Adele asked. 'Anything exciting?'

'Football. Talking to my mates at the bus stop,' Marcus said. 'That's about it.'

'Who are your mates, then?' Adele asked.

Marcus thought about it. 'Jamil, Horse, Ira—'

'Why's he called Horse?' Adele interrupted.

'Why's he doing what?'

'Horse. You said Horse. Why's he called that?'

'Dunno. He's always been called Horse.'

'What are they like?'

He shrugged. 'I dunno.' Marcus thought. How could he describe them? 'Jamil is gangly and walks like he has springs in every bone of his body. He can back-flip off a wall all day and never get tired.'

'Cool.'

'Sanjay has big, soft hands, two big feet, a face that's perfectly round, like a clock, and he's the fastest at running backwards and the best arm wrestler. Andrew is like … he strolls. Even when he's running, he looks like he's strolling.'

As he was talking Marcus could tell Adele wasn't really listening. She was nodding in the wrong places and looking into his eyes like she was giving him an eyesight test. He didn't really mind. Even he wasn't listening to himself much either, his mouth was moving but he was considering how he liked the curious little mark below her bottom lip on the right hand side. And her eyes were a sparkly green like the Westfield swimming pool tiles. He found himself drowning in them and his whole body went hot.

Abdul was stood over them again. 'Last of the big spenders you two, eh?' he said.

Marcus bought another coffee and another coffee milkshake. That was his bus fare gone.

'Where do you live?' he asked her.

'Roeville. We have a mansion by the river.'

She said it in an off-hand way, like it meant nothing.

'And a flash car,' Marcus added. 'You're loaded, aren't you?'

'It's all appearances,' Adele said.

What did that mean? Marcus thought. But he let it go. 'What's this secret you had to tell me about then?' he asked.

She gave him her sideways glance. 'Can I trust you?'

'Course.'

'You won't tell My Talented Brother?'

'I never see him unless it's a match.'

'The lift they gave you, didn't you think it was a bit strange?'

'Not really.'

'They're trying to discover your secret. You know what I mean? How you can play so good.'

'He can come practice with us if he wants.' That was it? Marcus thought. All this rushing, just for that?

'Dad reckons that if they can stop you playing, they'll win the league. That was why they picked you up, to find out how to stop you.'

Marcus pulled a face. He didn't believe her.

'He said something else,' Adele continued.

'What?'

'I'll tell you another time,' she said, gathering her bags. 'I've got to run. My girls will be waiting for me. Text me and we'll meet up again. If you want,' she said.

Marcus shrugged.

Adele stood, moved to go, and turned around again.

'One last thing,' she said.

'What's that?'

'You need a shower!' She stuck her tongue out at him. Then she dashed off, trailing bags.

Marcus watched her leave. She'd insulted him about needing a shower, so why was he grinning?

THE DOG THING

It was Sunday afternoon. Nobody was in. Marcus flung his boots bag on the sofa, slapped together a peanut butter sandwich then went out and practiced cushioned volleys in the alley. When the volleys were bang on, he decided to try half volleys. The first one he tried, he *almost* landed it. The ball flew up along the alley and landed in the corner house neighbour's back yard.

'To rass,' he muttered to himself, then 'just my flippin luck.'

This neighbour kept a Rottweiler on a long chain in the yard. Marcus knew the dog well. It had the deepest bark Marcus had ever heard, and came charging to the back gate in a vicious snarl when anyone passed. Now it had his Adidas Teamfeist Capitano. The owner refused to return anything. Everyone in the neighbourhood called it the football graveyard. But it was not going to be his football's graveyard. Besides the half volleys, curls and layoffs he still had to practice, no way was he giving up his ATC.

Marcus ran back along the alley and ducked into his own yard. The kitchen door was still open. He found what he was looking for on the top shelf of the fridge then hurried out again.

Scrambling up onto the back wall of the Rottweiler's yard was no problem. Marcus tried to hold his balance there, but the top of the wall was old and crumbly. The bricks shifted under his trainers. There was a furious rumble of dog and chain as the Rottweiler leapt for him, its teeth glinting, and its mouth full of slobber. As it leapt, Marcus threw it a piece of cooked sausage. The dog twisted mid-leap to snap at the sausage. It missed first time, but turned, adjusted in mid-air, snapped again and caught it, chopping it in two. The Rottweiler landed on the ground with his chain flailing, and it gobbled the last bit of sausage. It liked it. It hunched low, coiled. Marcus readied for the dog to attack once more, but it didn't. Its barking stopped. Marcus watched. The dog's tail wagged. And its ears were pricked high. Suddenly he understood. The dog was waiting for the next piece of sausage. 'Sit!' Marcus commanded. The dog sat. Its wide slobbering mouth panted.

Despite its size, it was a skinny thing, Marcus noticed; the owner probably wasn't feeding it right. He spotted his ATC by the drainpipe under the kitchen window. Five other balls lay in the yard, burst and muddy with age. The dog was still sitting. It scratched the earth with its paws, wriggled on its bum then raised itself off its haunches in anticipation of more sausage.

'Sit!' Marcus said again. The dog settled once more.

Slowly Marcus lowered himself into the yard. The dog stood. Marcus threw the sausage into a far corner. The dog hurtled round and followed it. Marcus dashed across and grabbed his ball. He turned to climb the wall again. Too late. The dog was done with the sausage and had cut him off. Marcus put his hand in his pocket. There was no more sausage, but the dog did not know that, he thought.

'Sit!' he ordered once more, keeping his hand in his pocket.

The dog sat.

He had read somewhere that dogs could smell fear. Marcus threw back his head, stuck out his chest and walked past the Rottweiller like he owned the yard. The dog lowered its head as he passed, and sniffed him. Calmly, Marcus hauled himself up the wall. When he turned back, the dog was still sitting, whining pleadingly.

'Good boy,' Marcus said, 'I'll be back.'

He jumped down into the alley, dashed back to his kitchen, raided the fridge again, ran out and climbed the wall. The dog did not bark this time. It was already sitting, its tail wagging. Marcus threw it another piece of sausage. It gobbled up the meat, turned and sat again.

'Good boy,' said Marcus.

He threw another morsel and jumped into the yard as the dog chewed it. Marcus rescued four of the other balls, even though they were all badly mangled. He left one ball, the most chewed one, for the dog to play with.

He went up to the dog, and felt its collar and found the silver disc that dangled there. It was engraved with one word. Nero.

'Nero?' he said.

The dog looked up at him, still chomping on sausage.

'Good boy, Nero.'

Nero stopped chewing. His ears pricked up and his head swung round towards his house.

Suddenly the back door opened and the owner was out in the backyard with them.

'What are you doing in my yard?' the owner shouted at Marcus. He was tall and had wild hair, scruffy trousers and what looked like newspaper stuffed into the sleeves of his woolly grey jumper.

The dog was between them.

'Sorry, I came for my ball,' Marcus said.

'That dog'll rip you to pieces and it'll be your own fault!' the owner said, sawing the air with his hands as he said it.

Nero growled. More at the owner than at Marcus though, Marcus thought.

'Sorry,' Marcus said. 'I'll go now.'

He leaped onto the wall, leaped off it into the alleyway and ran back home. Later that night, his mum moaned about him eating too much, that they couldn't afford it, and she'd have to put a lock on the fridge door if it carried on. She was on the computer as she said this, searching for websites of rival double-glazing companies. His dad grunted a hello. He had taken the photograph of Marcus's grandfather off the wall and was staring at it. 'He was a chief you know,' Marcus's dad said to him, as Marcus headed to his room.

'I know, Dad,' Marcus sighed. 'You've told me enough times.'

ACTIONS HAVE CONSEQUENCES

There were four chairs outside the head of year's office. One of the chairs had a dead beetle on it. Two of them were wet from a roof leak. He sat on the fourth. He had been hauled out of Monday form class by a teaching assistant and escorted here. He waited. Eventually the teaching assistant emerged from the office and waved him in, before scuttling away down the corridor.

Marcus entered and looked around. He'd been here a few times before. The same certificates in frames on the wall behind the desk, the same bag of golf clubs in a corner, the same 'You-Don't-Have-To-Be-Crazy-To-Work-Here-But-It-Helps' mug on his table by the keyboard. That same 'shame-on-you' look on the head of year's face.

'I'll keep this short, Marcus,' Ozone said. 'Actions have consequences. Walking out of Miss Podborsky's class has to be punished.'

Ozone's hairspray afro shook with sternness. Yet something in his tone told Marcus that the head of year himself was not fully committed to what he was saying.

'But why, Sir?'

'Cause and effect. Understand?'

'No, Sir.' Marcus imagined the gold Buddha that his mum kept on her bedroom mantelpiece. 'Calm. Be calm,' he thought.

'For every action there is an equal and opposite reaction. You know that. Marcus. Year 8 Physics. So the consequences are these. I'm suspending you from the school football team.'

'What?! Sir?! That's nuts.'

Marcus suddenly remembered Mr Davies's heated conversation on the touchline with Ozone. So this was what it was about.

'I'm not going to argue about it,' said Ozone. 'My decision is made.'

'But that's crazy, Sir. That's the stupidest thing I can imagine. What has football got to do with geography, Sir?'

'Don't dig yourself another hole, Marcus. Watch your lip.'

'Stuff you,' he thought, 'and stuff the football team!' Marcus stormed off. He heard Ozone calling him back. He slammed Ozone's door on him. He'd had enough. He wanted to destroy something. He walked along corridor after corridor. Bells rang, people pushed past him. Someone even slapped him on the back. None of it meant anything to him. In his mind was the burning injustice of what had happened. To take away from him the one thing that he loved, the one thing that made the rest of school bearable, it was like they were trying to kill him.

Going home was useless. Mum would only be mad at him for getting in trouble at school again then she would be too busy breastfeeding Leah, worrying about Leah's cold and puzzling why the radiator in Leah's room didn't work properly. His dad, if he was home, would be lost in a dream world, gargling his larynx-strengthening brews, writing headlines in his warped imagination:

EXCLUSIVE! THE PART-TIME POSTMAN WHO TOOK THE POP WORLD BY STORM!

EXCLUSIVE! PART-TIME POSTIE WITH THE GOLDEN TONSILS GOES GLOBAL!

He hated school and everyone in it. Why could they not put him on report like every other kid who misbehaved? They'd invented a punishment just for him.

Someone made a grab for his ATC. He pushed him away. Someone else jumped into his face and laughed. Others were smiling as they chatted on their way to their next class. They didn't know what he knew, he thought, which was that this school was a tyranny. Suddenly Leonard was in his face. 'What's up, Marcus?', he said, all glee, 'had some bad news?' Marcus remembered how Leonard had been sneaking around on the touchline when Ozone was quarrelling with the coach. It dawned on him that Leonard had known all along this was going to happen. And hadn't warned him. Marcus lunged for Leonard. Leonard shot into a classroom and held the door fast. Marcus struck the glass with his fist. His fist bounced off the glass. All the school glass was toughened now. Behind the glass, Leonard grinned inanely at him. 'Calm. Be calm', Marcus told himself. He gave up on Leonard. For now.

He sat down in a stairwell. Tears blocked his eyes and he fought to blink them back. How could he deserve this? He had not sworn at Miss Podborsky. He had not thrown anything at her. He had simply walked out. Nobody wanted to hear his side of the story. No one wanted to know that Miss Podborsky was picking on him, and she kept doing it.

His eyes were burning. He saw a fire exit. He ran to it, whacked the fire exit bar down so the steel doors swung open, and stepped out. The air felt good: cold and fresh. The school gates were a hundred metres away.

The playground was empty. He saw the tarmac exit road that snagged past the car park. The school's high iron gates were swung fully back. He knew that the CCTV would cover the gates, and he'd be suspended from school for truancy, but it didn't matter now. The wet tarmac shimmered. He looked up at the sky then he ran. The wind scooped him up and propelled him along the tarmac, past the car park. He was about to burst through the gates, to freedom, when he heard a shout at his shoulder.

'Marky! Wait!'

It was Horse. Horse's huge legs staggered as he ran, like they were going to buckle. Marcus stopped. Horse leaned on him while he got his breath back. His panting slowly became deep breaths.

'Where. Are. You … Going?'

'Out of here.'

'What's up?'

Marcus shook his head. He knew he'd cry if he tried to talk.

'C'mon, bro.'

Marcus shook his head again.

'Hey, it's me, Horse. I got your back.' Horse's face was so close into his own their eyebrows almost rubbed.

51

Marcus pulled away. He fought back tears. Anyway, what could Horse do? Diddly squat. He started walking again.

'Don't do it, Marky, don't!' Horse flung himself at him, stuck his head into Marcus's chest, clamped his arms around him and squeezed Marcus, tugging him left, then right.

Ordinarily, if anybody attacked Marcus like that, Marcus would have fought him off, even Horse. It wasn't physical strength Marcus lacked, it was energy. He let Horse wrestle him to the ground.

'See?' Horse grunted, when they both tumbled down. Horse sat right on top of him and pinned Marcus's arms to the tarmac. 'I got the strength of three men,' Horse said, 'Don't mess with me. Don't get me mad. Ha! I'm like the Incredible Hulk! I'm gonna rip off my shirt next!'

That was ridiculous, Marcus thought, so ridiculous it was funny.

'You're smiling now, Marky, you smiled,' Horse said. 'C'mon. Nothing's ever that bad. What's got you messed up, bro'?'

Marcus sat up and told Horse what had happened. 'It's sick,' Marcus said, 'they're messing with my head. I can't take it. Why?'

'I seen Miss Podborsky pick on you. It's like you're the cleverest black kid in the class, hell you are the cleverest kid in the class. And she don't like it. She's a racist, bro.'

'But why?'

'There's no why to racism. It just is. But you know, we all on your side. You're representin' us, know what I'm saying? And we got you.' Horse scratched his head and eased his legs. 'We can fight back.'

'What do you mean?'

'I'm on the School Council. I can raise it there.'

'C'mon. That's litter-picking and recycling.'

Horse jumped up. 'I know! A petition! We'll get a piece of paper with everyone's name on it saying we object. That'll do it. The whole team. If everyone signs, they'll have to give in. Else it will be like the French Revolution. Off with their heads! We can say we won't play unless they put you back on the team. A strike!'

Horse's enthusiasm was infectious. 'You think they'll listen?' Marcus asked. 'Ropey Face and Ozone?'

'It's worth a try. Come on,' Horse said, standing up. 'We'll find the others, get them to sign up. If we rush back, we'll hardly be late. It's art. Miss Siddique always forgets to take the register. No one will hardly have noticed.'

They sneaked into art and their luck was in, the register was still sitting on Miss Siddique's desk. Somehow news of Marcus's suspension from the team had already got around. At playtime, most of the team said they'd sign the petition. Only Leonard refused, saying it was Marcus's own fault he'd got suspended.

The last lesson of the day was PE. As they got changed for basketball, Horse went round to get the last few names on the petition. Mr Davies came out of his office and walked up to Marcus.

'That's enough, Marcus,' he said, loud enough so everyone heard. 'I know this hurts. Half an hour ago I was in Mr Wrexham's office and told him not to do this, especially its timing, I begged him, but he refused to budge.'

The whole team had gathered and was listening. The atmosphere in the changing room was rebellious, torch paper waiting for a match.

'So your petition's not going to work,' continued Mr Davies. He turned round and talked to everyone. 'Horse, you'll make a great trade unionist one day, but you have to pick your fights. A petition's not going to work. But we can still win the game. We can. And you'd want us to win it, wouldn't you, Marcus? After all the work we've all put in: All the training in the freezing cold, David training on his birthday, Ahmed missing a funeral, Sanjay breaking his nose and playing on? You'd want us to win after all that, wouldn't you?'

'Of course,' said Marcus awkwardly.

'So let's get a grip,' Mr Davies rallied. 'Tell your parents there's a special practice session tomorrow. I've worked out some new tactics. Leonard, are you here?'

'Yes,' Mr Davies.

Leonard came forward. His pleasing smile firmly in place.

'Right,' said Mr Davies. 'We're going to slot Leonard into Marcus's place in midfield, see how it works.'

'The traitor,' Marcus thought, 'the only one who hadn't signed the petition.'

'Marcus, we need you there tomorrow even though you're not playing. Be another set of eyes for me. Are we all good?'

There were vague murmurs of yes.

'Listen, we can still win this league. Come on,' Mr Davies called out. 'Are we up for it? Yes?'

'Yes!' went someone meekly.

'Are we up for it?' the coach fired, he sounded wounded now, like he wished he hadn't started this cheering thing.

Leonard jumped up on a bench. 'Yes! Yes! Yes!' The noise grew as one by one the team joined in with him.

Leonard's smooth face and smart air-punching roused them like a top politician at a rally. By the time he was done, he had Horse and everyone cheering to the rafters. As the din swelled to its loudest, Leonard turned and looked down at Marcus. In the middle of his face was a wide smirk. Then he laughed in Marcus's face. Marcus showed him one slow middle finger. Leonard turned his back on him and whipped the frenzy up even higher. They all piled out of the changing rooms in high spirits, slapping each other's backs. All except Marcus.

Marcus dawdled. On the floor, he spotted his torn, muddy, discarded petition. He picked it up, crushed it into a sodden mass then flung it down again. He texted Adele.

LATE NIGHT PENALTIES

The school bell went for home time. Everyone swarmed past Marcus, chasing for the buses, running for friends, waving to parents in cars. Marcus started for home, alone. A heavy rain began falling but he avoided the bus stop. He liked the rain. It took him thirty minutes to get to his house and he was drenched when he got to the door. His bag was soaked, his shoes squelched, his clothes stuck to him. His mum tried to give him a hug but he shrugged her off.

'What's the matter?' she asked.

He ignored her and she went back to practicing her magic circle card tricks. His dad was in his headphones, miming music with his lips like a goldfish. Only Leah seemed to care. She gave Marcus an extra big smile when he picked her up and she cooperated for once when he fed her.

After tea, he sloped off to the bus stop by the primary school playground. Adele sent him a text saying she wanted to meet up. He gave her the street name of the school. His spirits lifted. The sky thundered as he walked along, but it didn't rain. He juggled his ATC up to the bus stop. As luck would have it, Leonard was there, with Horse and Jamil. Leonard was stood up, doing most of the talking. The sound of Leonard's voice had Marcus grinding his teeth. He sat down on a spare seat. Horse came and stood by Marcus, Horse's back leaning against the glass of the bus shelter.

'The thing is,' Leonard was saying, 'it's a matter of tactics. Most of these matches are close …'

Marcus listened sceptically, missing words here and there, but not caring. Getting the nod from Mr Davies had filled Leonard's lungs and swelled his head, Marcus thought.

'… and it's often a penalty that decides the game,' Leonard continued, 'so that's what we need to practice. Penalties.'

'Unless we get played off the park,' Jamil said.

'Mr Davies already told me we can beat them. And we can, with the right tactics. Isn't that right, Marcus?' asked Leonard.

'What do I know, Lenny?' Marcus replied. 'You seem to have got it all worked out anyway.'

Why was Leonard suddenly the team leader? Marcus thought. He was only a sub. That meant there were at least eleven players better than him. What did the others see in him, listening to him like this?

'There is a way, Bowker are not unbeatable,' Leonard resumed. 'So let us say, for the sake of argument, it comes down to who sticks the ball in the net from twelve yards when the whistle for full time blows. Now I've done some research and …'

Leonard was a smooth talker. By the time he had finished speaking, everyone had agreed to practice penalties.

'Marcus, since you won't be playing, you can be referee,' Leonard said, holding out a whistle.

Marcus shook his head in disbelief, yet took the whistle off him. They climbed over the primary school railings and scrambled through the thick bushes into the field. The goalposts in the primary school field were not full scale ones, but Leonard said it didn't matter, the technique was the same.

Each of them took turns to be goalkeeper. By the end of four rounds, everyone had missed a penalty except Leonard. By round ten, Leonard was three strikes ahead of his nearest rival, Jamil. Everyone was impressed, even Marcus, though he made sure he didn't show it.

'You want to know how it's done?' Leonard, called out. There was no answer. 'Well, I'm gonna tell you anyway!' That made them laugh. They were eating out of Leonard's hand, Marcus thought, Leonard was now Prime Minister, Top Comedian and Star Football Manager all rolled into one.

'It's in the eyes,' Leonard said. 'You look one way, shoot the other. The goalkeeper always goes the wrong way.' He showed them how he did it. 'When ... wait a minute,' Leonard said, turning suddenly and looking into the gathering dark. 'You see someone there?' he said, 'by the bushes?'

Everyone turned, startled.

'Hey!' Leonard called out.

Nothing moved. Everything looked normal.

'Right there!' Leonard insisted, pointing into the gloom. It looked like two bin bags in the bushes at the railings by the gate.

Everyone stared. Suddenly the bags moved. A shadow stood forward of the outline of bushes.

Marcus recognised the silhouette instantly. *Adele.* He waved her over.

'Is she who I think she is?' Leonard called to Marcus, as Adele neared them.

There were giggles from Jamil and Horse.

'Depends who you think she is,' replied Marcus. Adele was standing next to him now.

'The Bowker Vale captain's sister?'

'My name's Adele.'

More giggles from Horse and Jamil.

'She's a spy,' said Leonard.

'She isn't,' Marcus snapped.

'I'm not. I was just trying to surprise him,' said Adele.

Leonard ignored her. 'Then what was she doing there?' he said to Marcus. 'Why was she watching us from the bushes? If that's not spying, what is? Is she your girlfriend?' he pressed.

Everyone was waiting. Marcus felt daft trying to explain. So he simply said, 'Yes.'

Jamil whooped, Horse slapped his thighs.

Leonard snorted. 'That's nice, I'm happy for you both. But she can't watch.'

'Why? I don't see the harm.' It was Horse.

'Let me explain,' said Leonard, placing his hands together like the Head at assembly. 'We're talking tactics. Tactics are most effective if they are unknown to the opposition. And she's got a hotline to the opposing team's captain. Sisters and brothers tell each other everything.'

'She might not,' said Horse.

'True, *might* not. But this is going to be the biggest match we've ever played, maybe the biggest in the history of the school. We can't take that risk. Right?' Leonard looked round to the others for support. They all nodded. 'Understand now, Horse?' Leonard asked, all nicey-nicey.

Horse looked across at Marcus and then shuffled the ball at his feet. Marcus felt sorry for him. He could see his dilemma, to side with Leonard and the rest of the team, or with him.

The weather decided for them all. Thunder smashed across the sky and rain fell in huge dollops. They ran for the cover of the bus stop shelter. By the time the rain eased, everyone was chatting about all kinds of stuff and Marcus slipped away with Adele.

SPY TRIAL

'Are you a spy?' Marcus asked. They were walking along the primary school road, side by side. Their hands had brushed a couple of times, but they'd not actually held hands.

'Yes, I am,' Adele said, spinning round to look him right in the face. 'I've got a spy hat and secret writing ink under the stairs.'

Marcus tried again. 'Did Anthony or your dad ask you to come here?'

'Okay, stupid. What would I report? "Six lads running around in the rain." That's hardly gonna get me a spy medal is it?'

It was like wrestling with an eel, Marcus thought. Not that he had actually wrestled any eels. 'Why did you come then?'

Adele looked at him. She was about to say one thing, he could see it in the dance of her eyes. But she said something else.

'Dad wanted me out of the house. They're both talking about you non-stop. You are "A-Phenomenon", I don't get it. They see the Lady Gaga of football, I see some sweaty boy with a … ball at his feet. Anyway I've got good news for you.'

'What's that?' said Marcus, sceptical.

Her hand was resting in his now as they walked. He didn't know how that had happened.

'The Bowker Vale coach has got cancer and can't do the team anymore. My dad thinks he can step in. And if my dad steps in, it will be all about Anthony.'

'So you're a spy, but you're a spy for us?' Marcus said, swinging her hand a little.

'Or maybe I'm a double agent?' Adele said. 'Pretending to spy for you but really spying for them? Or pretending to spy for them, but really spying for you? Or a triple agent. Pretending to you that I'm pretending to spy for them and actually spying for you, but really I'm spying for them?'

Marcus tried to work it out. She had him all twisted up.

'And if I'm a spy,' she smiled, 'that makes you James Bond, don't it?' She nudged him in the ribs.

Marcus liked that. He saw himself as more Will Smith than James Bond, but nevertheless.

'Isn't there a film called *The Spy Who Loved Me*?' she asked.

Now he knew she was teasing him. He flicked water off a wet tree leaf at her, then chased her.

THE PROPERTIES OF MATTER AND ANTI-MATTER

It was the final practice session before the match that would decide who won the schools league. Mr Davies was in the middle of the pitch. His brow was furrowed, his head down. 'Alright, let's concentrate. Where's the bibs, Leonard? Two teams. Red team. Green team. Red team is …' The coach called out six names. 'Blue team is …' He called out another six names.

'Which one am I?' asked Marcus. He hadn't heard his name.

'Red. Over here. Marcus, are you looking at me?'

Marcus nodded.

'You've got a special job today. You're the canary.'

'What?'

'Listen,' the coach said, putting an arm around him. 'In the old days, they sent a canary down coal mines in a cage, to test for gas. If it came back up dead, the miners knew not to go there.'

'So I'm going to end up dead?'

'Don't be soft.'

'What then?'

'You're going to be Anthony Vialli. And our midfield's going to practice tackling you. It will be rough, but, if you pick up a little knock here in practice it won't matter because you're not playing.'

'I'm expendable?'

'I wouldn't put it like that, but yeah, for today. Now listen you're Anthony, their key player, the ugly one with the bent nose, you know him, right?'

Marcus nodded, smiling. Somehow Mr Davies could always get under his skin, even when he was trying hard to sulk.

'Leonard, Horse and the green bib rabble, are us, Ducie. So Bowker's Anthony gets the ball. How do we stop him playing? Horse and Leonard are going to be looking to get the tackle in. Understand so far, heard everything?'

Marcus nodded.

'Right. What would you do if you was Anthony and you've got Horse and Leonard on tow, middle of the pitch?'

'I'm dropping deeper, get away from them and get the ball,' Marcus replied.

'Fine, takes the canary out of the danger zone. Next question. Horse or Leonard. Who's going to give you more grief?'

'Horse is twice the size. Leonard's faster on his feet. I can lose Horse, not Leonard. But Leonard can't hurt me.'

'Okay, thanks Marcus, let's see how it goes.' Mr Davies blew his whistle and gathered everyone around to explain the exercise. The pitch was going to be narrowed, the goalposts were cones. And it was midfield versus midfield.

'We're coming for you!' warned Horse. He linked arms conspiratorially with Leonard.

'Got to catch me first,' replied Marcus. Horse wouldn't get anywhere near him, he was sure.

Everyone took their places. The coach blew. The reds played the ball from the back and made the pass to Marcus. Horse steamed in. Marcus vaulted over Horse's first scything tackle. Leonard followed in, both feet flying, and caught Marcus's thigh with studs. Marcus fell to the turf.

For a moment, Leonard stood above him, grinning. Then he stepped away to high-five with Horse.

A thin line of blood oozed out of Marcus's thigh. It was just a scrape.

'Again!' the coach called.

The ball came to Marcus again. He dropped a shoulder, sending Horse the wrong way. Leonard came steaming in. Marcus trapped the ball between his heels and hoiked it into the air, carrying the ball and himself over Leonard's high tackle. He dropped down and flighted the ball perfectly to Jamil, who smashed it between the green's cones.

'Only you, Marcus!' shouted Mr Davies, 'Nobody else could pull that trick! Alright, again!'

This time Marcus lost Horse easily. He slipped Leonard with a trick called a flip-flap, then zoomed the ball to Jamil again. He'd bamboozled Leonard so badly this time that Leonard had fallen over. It was Marcus's turn to grin.

'Alright, forget zonal,' called Mr Davies. 'Horse, swap with Leonard, Leonard, man to man on Marcus, stick to him like chewing gum ... soon as he gets the ball ... the tackle in, annihilate him. Like you're his anti-matter. Wallop! Let's go!'

Before the ball had even come to Marcus, Leonard grabbed Marcus's shirt. Just as Marcus was about to cry foul, Leonard let go of the shirt. Suddenly released, Marcus over-ran the ball. Leonard got it and walloped it away.

'He had my shirt!' Marcus protested.

'Get over it,' Mr Davies shouted to him. 'Football's not a game for fairies, that's badminton!' Mr Davies imitated a badminton player wafting the air. Everyone laughed. 'Good work, Leonard,' the coach continued, 'let's go again.'

This time, as Leonard tried to grab his shoulder, Marcus shoved Leonard off him, broke clear and collected the ball. He turned to pass only for Leonard to slide through him, slicing off his shin guard and dumping Marcus on his backside. Marcus looked at his leg. Blood oozed from his left shin again, the old injury. He'd seen the look as Leonard had slid in. Leonard had deliberately reopened the wound he'd picked up in the semi-final.

'Idiot!' Marcus muttered at Leonard.

'Way to go, Leonard!' called out Mr Davies.

Leonard was right on Marcus's shoulder. 'Bleed easy, don't you?' Leonard said to him.

Marcus ignored him. He turned away, looking for the ball. Concentration.

'You're a wuss,' Leonard continued. 'Crying in Miss Podborsky's ...? A big girl. Waaa!'

Marcus felt his face heat up. He turned. 'What?'

'What? Can't hear can you either? Eh? Eh? Eh?'

That was it. Marcus swung a fist at Leonard's face.

He missed but Leonard still fell to the grass and rolled. Marcus fell on him.

Then Mr Davies was between them, shouting. 'Hey, Marcus, Marcus, don't take it personal, it's an exercise.' Mr Davies held them apart.

'He's opened my shin up again. He's hit it three times tonight,' Marcus said.

'Coincidence,' Leonard smirked from the ground where he'd stopped rolling to reveal his perfectly unmarked face.

'C'mon, boys, no need for handbags at dawn. Marcus, keep cool. Leonard, well done, good job. You got him riled, as I asked. Do that in the match with Anthony and it'll wreck his rhythm. Okay. Again!'

Leonard was the sneakiest player on the pitch, Marcus decided. If he wasn't pulling his shirt, tugging his shorts, chatting shit in his ear, then he was blocking his view or standing on his foot. When all of that failed, Leonard simply clattered him and conceded the foul. Mr Davies loved everything Leonard did. Going deeper had no effect, Leonard simply followed him. It was a battle. Marcus learned to face Leonard rather than have him at his back, and to push off him at the last moment before he got the ball. Then, when he collected it, Marcus controlled it and passed it first touch.

Slowly, Marcus's one-touch moves began to make Leonard look clumsy. When, in six attempts one after the other, Marcus escaped Leonard and made the pass to Jamil, everyone could see Marcus had the beating of him.

'Chin up, Leonard,' Mr Davies rallied, as Leonard's head dropped. 'Anthony Vialli can't play tight like Marky, you'll eat Anthony alive, Leonard. Keep on!'

Finally Leonard hacked Marcus down in the middle of the pitch, with the ball nowhere near them, right on the left shin injury. Marcus fell to the ground, clutching his leg. Leonard stood over him. 'Fairy!'

'Alright, alright!' called the coach, over them fast. 'Jamil take Marcus's place. Marcus lose that frown, Leonard's only carrying out orders. Easy on Jamil, Leonard, we need him for the match. And don't bother with the verbals any more, you're just too good, Lenny!'

'He calls *me* a fairy and he's going to Neverland!' proclaimed Jamil, fists high. 'I'll smack him that hard!'

Everyone laughed, even Leonard.

Marcus limped off and the session went on without him. He was bruised all over. His left sock was soaked red with blood. He stood alone by the side of the training grid, watching Leonard call all the shots and the coach love Leonard for it.

THE LEAGUE DECIDER

Marcus was on the touchline, shuffling his feet. He hated it there. He belonged in the centre of the pitch, where Leonard was now. The wind was clipping his neck, whipping in from the other side. Over on that side, he could make out Mr Vialli, giving it large with a clipboard and a stopwatch. So Adele was right about that one, her dad had taken over as Bowker coach. He missed Adele. He remembered her fooling around in the car the first time they'd met. The Bowker team was all around Mr Vialli. Marcus spotted among them Dwayne and Mohammad, two of the Bowker players he had teamed up with at Summer School. Around the Bowker players were a bunch of keen parents, two Labradors and a Chihuahua. Adele spotted Marcus looking and waved. Marcus waved back quickly. He wanted her to run over to him but he knew that was not on. He quickly texted her a 'hiya' instead. Then he looked along the Ducie touchline.

Mr Davies was next to Marcus in his sleeping-bag-coat-thing, talking with the Manchester United scout. A stray dog appeared to be listening in. 'Have you ever seen a better pitch?' Mr Davies was saying. 'Look at that semi-circle, we re-turfed it, same with the goal-line and the penalty spot zones. We've had the …ker up and down it for …age, then rollered it. See how level it is? Got to … the best pitch in the schools league or my name's not Larry.'

The stray dog sniffed Mr Davies's bottom half-heartedly.

'It looks a good pitch, Mr Davies,' the scout smiled, 'Why's Marcus … playing?'

Mr Davies scowled, swiping at the dog behind him. 'Disciplinary matters. I begged the head of year, but he's a sandwich short, doesn't understand football at all. One point … the league's ours for the first time in a decade, yet he pulls our best player – sabotage. Like I say, a sandwich short, between you and me. You've got to give leeway with the council estate kids, lower your expectations; parents' chaotic lifestyles and all that.' Mr Davies's eyebrows wiggled to emphasise the point.

The coach turned to Marcus. '… discipline issue, Marcus?'

Marcus was about to open his mouth, but Mr Davies's wiggling eyebrows jumped in before he could say anything.

'You know what they're like at this age, the hormones. They kick off over anything. Marcus slammed a door too loud, something like that, and he's very sorry. Right, Marcus?'

Marcus nodded.

The scout kissed his teeth. 'Pull this guy from your team on the eve of a league decider? By my standards he'd had to have murdered someone.'

'Like I said, a sandwich short, the head of year is,' Mr Davies agreed. 'The new kid's good though. Watch him. Leonard. It's a more defensive line-up. We only need one point. We've got tactics. It's the Christmas tree formation, but without the baubles. Leonard's slotted right in. We've been through it in training, we can do this. Right, Marcus?'

Marcus duly nodded.

The scout checked his watch and Mr Davies became even more eager. 'Got my full set of coaching badges this summer … appointments arise, I'm your man. I left Bowker for Ducie, you know. I wasn't sacked for poor results, despite what they say. Left for the toughest council estate school in the borough. Tougher challenge. And it's come good now, just watch. When it comes to coaching I'm up there, though I say so myself. Ready for the next challenge. If Man United want me, even in a part-time or voluntary capacity for their youth teams …'

'Well, good luck, Mr Davies,' said the scout, cutting him short. He shook Mr Davies's hand then offered his hand to Marcus, to Marcus's surprise. Marcus turned away, flipped his ATC onto his head and balanced it there.

'Please yourself,' the scout said. 'Tell you what, Mr Davies,' the scout shouted, 'that boy can sulk!'

Mr Davies mouthed 'stupid boy' silently at him. Marcus ignored Mr Davies and watched the scout make his way across the pitch to where the Bowker Vale camp were gathered. Only the stray dog remained with Marcus and Mr Davies on the Ducie touchline.

Marcus's phone vibrated. He checked it. From Adele:

Hiya ☺

It pulled Marcus's mood up a bit. The whistle went. Bowker kicked off. The game started tentatively, both teams finding their feet. Leonard slammed a tackle in, collected the ball, fed it to Horse. Horse skidded in the mud, steadied himself, turned and flighted it high up in the air towards the Bowker Vale goalmouth. Jamil jumped and, if he'd reached it with his head, it might have gone in.

'Nice try, Jamil, keep it up!' yelled Mr Davies, by Marcus' side. 'Horse, more like that! We've got them on the run!'

Slowly, Bowker began to assert themselves. Marcus watched as, in the way that Marcus had predicted, the Bowker captain, Anthony dropped further back in midfield to lose his zone marker and collect the ball. Then, although he never went past anybody, Anthony did the simple pass well and made himself available for the return, moving Bowker up the pitch as he did so. His team responded to his prompts. They were brilliantly organised. Bowker started to look formidable. They held onto the ball. Ducie chased around uselessly.

'Leonard, what did I say? What's the plan? Shift it!' Mr Davies called out, exasperated.

Leonard galloped up the field and began man-marking Anthony, slamming into him whenever he received the ball and before he could choose his pass. Horse went with him, ready to follow up. The tactics suffocated the style out of Bowker and the game started turning in Ducie's favour again.

'They're not up for it, get in there!' Mr Davies called out.

Despite himself, Marcus had to admire the way Leonard and Horse worked. They were like hunting dogs. Their tackles were early and committed, just as they'd trained. Anthony was strangled totally out of the game.

On the other side of the pitch, Mr Vialli started yelling and waving his clipboard. Bowker stepped up their own tackling. Feet began flying everywhere. The new turf in the middle of the pitch soon lifted. Tiles of green began flying up in the air with the tackles.

Marcus watched as Mr Vialli paced up and down the opposite touchline in his suit, clipboard a-go-go, delivering instructions, and roaring his son on. Adele was by her dad, doing star jumps every time her brother made a pass. What if he'd been playing? Marcus thought, who would she have supported then? A whole row of Bowker dads were over there, patting players on the back if they came near the touchline. Marcus looked along their own touchline. The stray dog had left. There was nobody but Mr Davies and himself. Would his own dad have turned up if he'd been playing? Marcus asked himself. Fat chance. Adele waved to Marcus. Marcus did a short, embarrassed wave back, hoping no-one saw.

The referee blew his whistle and called the two captains over. One too many high tackles had gone in, he was warning them, Marcus could tell. The game calmed a little after that, with Bowker taking the upper hand. At half-time it was 0–0.

Mr Davies gave out orange pieces and told the team off. 'What's wrong with you lot? Nobody ate breakfast? Find your "On" button lads. Rocket's been waiting on the left wing. Bags of space. He's like a burglar looking at an open window. Give him the swag bag. Tony push up. Defence, you're sitting so far back you might as well be in bed. This match … ours for the taking. C'mon. Do the business! Marcus, get the water for them, how many times do I need to tell you? Leonard, we're still in this only because of you. Snap. Bite. Focus. Everyone, more like Lenny!'

Marcus seethed. Leonard the substitute was now Leonard the main man and he, Marcus, was reduced to handing out water.

At the start of the second half, Bowker picked up where they left off. They had placed their biggest tackler alongside Anthony Vialli as a minder and, with a nudge here and a push there, the minder stopped Leonard getting his tackles in. Marcus sniggered as he saw Leonard's frustration rise. With the tactic effective, the Bowker captain was free to distribute the ball where he liked. Marcus admired the precision of Anthony's play, he never misplaced a pass. The Bowker attacks were relentless. A heavy rain saved Ducie. It pounded the pitch, mixed in with the mud and started floating the grass turfs up again. The only way to get the ball moving was to kick it high in the air, above all the mud. Bowker Vale's pass-and-move game was useless. The pitch got so bad the referee called a halt and ordered all twenty two players to replace as many of the grass squares back into their holes in the pitch as they could. Then the ref came over to Mr Davies. 'Mr Davies, I trust the atrocious state of this pitch is not deliberate?'

'No, not … not at all. We had it re-laid especially,' Mr Davies stammered.

'Tsk. It's diabolical. I'll be making a report.'

Mr Davies muttered to himself as the referee returned to the centre of the pitch. The rain had stopped. The referee did a quick inspection of the repairs, declared himself satisfied and restarted the game with a drop ball. With the pitch restored, Bowker moved the ball around their team like they were one big pinball machine. Leonard charged around uselessly.

Mr Davies withdrew Jamil from attack to help Leonard get round Anthony's minder. Tackle after tackle slammed into Anthony, till the Bowker captain was hobbling. Marcus felt a little sorry for him. Horse slammed another tackle in that upended Anthony. It flung him in the air and dumped him hard on his backside. Marcus winced.

Mr Vialli had his arms out like a scarecrow, then flapped them like a bird, then clutched his chest, looking like his heart had stopped. All the time his mouth was in overdrive: 'Referee, have you forgotten your cards? That was an ambulance tackle! You'd better have insurance, matey!' Mr Vialli wagged a finger at the referee. Behind Mr Vialli, Adele giggled and star-jumped. Then she waved to Marcus again. He ignored her this time.

Anthony Vialli trotted over to his father on the touchline. A cloud of spray went up around him as his father applied Spray Ice all over his son's shins. Anthony came back on and began running without the hobble.

The referee showed four yellows over the next ten minutes and Mr Davies told Horse and Leonard to cool it, in case they got sent off. Bowker got their breath back.

Marcus bit his lower lip. Ducie were hanging on. In twelve minutes the match would be over. A draw would do for Ducie, they'd win the league. Only a win was good enough for Bowker though.

Anthony Vialli drove Bowker forward. He played three quick one-twos and found himself within five metres of the goal, the net staring at him, the ball at his feet. Marcus could only look through his fingers. Anthony drew back his sharp, left foot. Just as he was about to hammer the ball home, Horse slammed into him with a tackle that defied the laws of science by propelling

Anthony forwards and the ball backwards. The referee blew. 'Penalty! No tackling from behind!'

There was pandemonium. The referee waved all the protesting Ducie players away with a traffic policeman's icy glare and stiff hand, then, when things calmed, he reached into his upper pocket. He gave Horse a second yellow, quickly followed by a red card. Horse thought to say something. Mr Davies yelled like mad for him not to. Horse bit his tongue and sloped off. When he reached the touchline, he flung himself on the grass. Marcus bent down and put an arm around his neck. 'Hey, you did your best.'

'Wasn't good enough though, was it?' Horse muttered, accepting the water bottle Mr Davies offered him.

'C'mon, get up,' Marcus said, hauling Horse to his feet. 'There's a penalty on!' Together Marcus and Horse ran down the touchline to get a closer view of the penalty.

Anthony placed the ball on the spot. Luke, the Ducie keeper, smacked his gloves together and spat into them, then bounced up and down on the line, trying to make himself look bigger than he was. He had been the keeper since the start of Year 7, but for some reason he had not grown since then and was now looking a bit small compared to all the other players. But he was a brilliant gymnast, Marcus knew, and could jump higher than kids twice his size.

Anthony Vialli placed the ball on the front edge of the white circle that marked the penalty spot. He strode back. As he did so, he looked up at the sky and did the sign of a cross like a Catholic. He turned to face the goal, lowered his head, shuffled one measured step right then ran up and whacked the ball.

As he whacked it, his right foot slipped.

He hit the ball powerfully with his left foot.

The ball soared way over the cross-bar.

Anthony. Had. Missed.

Marcus' disbelieving eyes followed the ball soaring away like a kite. Cool headed Anthony Vialli. Marcus looked from the shrinking sphere in the sky to the player. Anthony was kneeling on the grass. He had a tile of turf in his hands and was pounding it into the ground in frustration. Mr Davies was doing a jig. Horse was whooping. Marcus joined in. Something else was kicking off on the pitch though. All three of them stopped and watched. The Bowker Vale players were surrounding the referee. Who was pedalling furiously backwards. From the Bowker touchline, Anthony's dad stormed onto the pitch and into the thick of it. Other Bowker parents followed him.

'No way, referee! No way!' Mr Vialli's big voice was booming. He had a square of turf in his hand and was waving it. It looked at one point like he was going to smash it over the referee's head. Marcus understood then what the protest was about. Bowker were blaming the loose turf. They wanted the kick taken again. It was too much for Marcus. He ran into the melee, Horse ran with him. Mr Davies ran after them. They joined the Ducie team protesting against the Bowker protests. The referee was still running backwards, waving everyone away, but he was out of puff now, and slowed to a stop, allowing himself to be surrounded. Mr Vialli stormed to the front of the Bowker players. He jabbed his big finger at the referee.

The referee blew his whistle, pointed to Mr Vialli and warned him: 'Cool it!'

Mr Vialli lost it completely: 'Cool it? You fat, blind, black bastard!'

Everyone startled and quietened.

Mr Vialli kept on. 'Call yourself a referee? My grandmother would make a better referee and she's six feet under! This is theft! You're stealing this game from us!'

Marcus couldn't believe his ears. Had Mr Vialli just said that? 'Black bastard'? It had changed the atmosphere. Everyone had fallen quiet. Mr Vialli looked around at them as if to say, 'what's up?'

The referee reached into his pocket. Marcus and the other players shrank away. Nobody wanted the next card. Marcus pulled at Horse to keep walking. The referee pulled out a Red from his top pocket. Who was it for? Nobody knew. From being surrounded, suddenly the referee had nobody within forty metres of him. The referee eyed his target, found it. He strode over to the Bowker touchline. Mr Vialli was there, suddenly busy punching numbers into his phone.

The referee stood in front of him and held the red card up high. 'You! Off! Off the grounds. Now!'

'Me? What have I done?!' Mr Vialli boomed.

'Off!' The referee was adamant.

Marcus watched as Mr Vialli shoved his phone in his tracksuit pocket and slunk off towards the car park. He saw Anthony wave briefly to his dad, then kick the turf in frustration. Meanwhile, Adele looked embarrassed and was scuffing her shoes. She didn't follow her dad off the field.

The referee blew again. 'The penalty is to be retaken!' he announced. 'It was incorrectly spotted first time.' He pointed to the Bowker end of the pitch. 'And this time it will be taken from this end! Any objections?'

The referee stared around. He had his hand on his top pocket like a gunslinger willing someone to make him draw.

The Ducie team stared at one another in disbelief. Had the referee gone potty? Was this even in the rule book? Could a penalty be retaken for that reason? And could you switch the taking of a penalty from one side of the pitch to another? Whatever they thought, with the referee in the mood he was in nobody dared object.

Luke, the Ducie keeper, made the long journey to the Bowker end. He stood between the posts where two minutes ago the Bowker keeper had been standing and smacked his gloves together. He spat into them then crouched to signal he was ready. The referee waved for the kick to be taken.

Anthony Vialli ran up. This time he made no mistake. He lashed the ball into the top, right side of the net, leaving Luke grabbing air on the left. Anthony turned, licked his finger and chalked up a 'One' on an imaginary board. His team mobbed him. The referee pointed to the centre spot. 1–0 to Bowker Vale.

Mr Davies went nuts. 'There's still time! There's still time! Leonard! Route One!'

Leonard tapped the ball from the kick-off towards Horse. Horse nudged past two of their players then hoofed the ball high for Jamil who had chased into the centre-forward position where Rocket usually was. Jamil leaped like a fish. Nobody had ever seen him leap so high. His springy legs catapulted him into the air. Their goalkeeper came out to punch it. His punch missed the ball and smacked Jamil square in the face.

Jamil rolled on the ground, clutching his eye. The referee blew again. 'Penalty!' Marcus gasped. It was a miracle. From despair to elation in less than fifteen seconds. Marcus jumped on Horse's back. Horse galloped up and down the touchline whooping. Mr Davies did a crazy war dance. Then they remembered Jamil. He was still flat out in the mud.

'Marcus grab the bucket!' Mr Davies ordered. The two of them ran over to Jamil. Marcus got there first. He plucked the sopping wet car sponge out of the plastic mop bucket and pushed it against Jamil's eye.

'What the heck!' spluttered Jamil, swinging a fist at Marcus, 'tryna drown me?' Marcus ducked, and pulled the sponge off him.

'We got the penalty?' Jamil asked, through his one good eye. He was still on his back on the turf.

'Yup,' said Marcus.

Jamil blinked his good eye. Marcus couldn't tell if this was meant to be a wink. Then Jamil said: 'It's mine. It's my goal. It's my penalty kick!'

'Don't be daft, Jamil, you've only got one eye,' Marcus told him 'and you don't even see good out of that.'

'I can see, I can see!' Jamil protested. But when he tried to get up, he was so dizzy he had to sit down again.

Who would take it? Marcus was sure if he had been playing, it would have been him. The ball was in a puddle on the pitch. He watched as Leonard went over and trapped it under his foot. Leonard picked it up and eyed the penalty spot. It was all in Leonard's hands. This kick could win them the league.

Leonard marched to the penalty spot with the ball tucked under his arm. He placed the ball carefully in the middle of the white paint and got the referee's nod that it was properly spotted. He walked back eight paces. He took one step to the left. Then he ran up. Marcus saw the slight turn of Leonard's head to his right, watched the ball sail low to the left. On target. Well struck. But their goalkeeper went the right way. He dived low and got something to it. Marcus couldn't see what, because Mr Davies had jumped into his view at the last moment. All he saw at the crucial moment was Mr Davies' sleeping-bag-coat and a patch of sky. But Mr Davies was now thumping the pitch. And Leonard was kneeling by the penalty spot, head low. And Bowker Vale were cheering and yelling like they'd all just won the Lottery. It all meant one thing. Leonard had missed.

Not ten seconds after the penalty kick was taken, a second after the Bowker Vale goalkeeper whacked the ball up the pitch, the referee blew his whistle. Full-time. It was over. Bowker Vale had won the league.

Nothing sickened Marcus more than watching Bowker celebrating. They did it loudly, all over the pitch and for a long time. Adele was star-jumping, Mr Vialli had magically reappeared with some party streamers that he was letting off. Then Bowker did some kind of a war dance in the middle of the Ducie pitch. Marcus turned his back and joined the Ducie team's slow march to the dressing room.

In the changing room, there was a long, awful silence. Some of the team shot Marcus angry looks as they kicked off their boots and slumped on the benches. Marcus felt awkward, unsure whether to stay or go. Horse squeezed his arm as he went by. In the back, the showers hissed, but nobody was showering.

Mr Davies broke the silence. 'Okay boys, listen up. Get rid of the long faces. I know you'll be thinking we could have won that match. A season of hard work come to nothing.' He sighed. 'All because some boy couldn't keep his temper in class!'

'Sod you!' Marcus flung the water bottle down, and ran towards the changing room doors.

'Hey, don't!' Horse wrestled Marcus back and sat with an arm around him, all Horse's weight holding him down.

'Sorry, Marcus,' said Mr Davies, 'but sometimes you have to hear hard things, it's part of the journey called life.' He looked around at all the team. 'And we can't put it all on Marcus' toes. There's plenty more "if onlys" if you go looking for them. "If only" Leonard had stuck that penalty in the back of the net. "If only" the referee hadn't let them retake their own penalty. "If only" our centre-halves hadn't lost concentration at the vital moment. "If only". There's no point in "if onlys". We lost. We. Lost. Past tense. It's over. We've got to look to the future. We have the cup final coming up soon. And we're going to win that, right?'

The team gave a reluctant shout of yes.

'C'mon. What are we going to do? Win, right? Say it with me, win! Let's hear it, win!'

'Win! Win! Win!' Everyone joined in this time. The shout was determined, and yet somehow gloomy.

'Okay, well done, that's the attitude,' Mr Davies said. 'Get showered, get dressed, go home and start focusing on that Cup final. Whose turn is it to take the kit home for washing? Leonard? Okay, everybody, throw your kit at Leonard!'

Leonard yelped as he got pelted with a dozen sweaty, dirty football kits. Somehow throwing their kit at him made them all feel better. Except Marcus. Glumly, he checked his phone. A text from Adele.

Sorry u lost. Amazing game. U wd av won if ud plyd ☺

Marcus texted back.

Yeh woteva

Later, when Marcus, Leonard, Horse and Jamil were all gathered at the bus stop, the gleaming Bowker Vale school van zoomed past them. The driver tooted as it went past and all the Bowker players made rude hand signs. Marcus and the Ducie players jeered back at them.

Their bus back to the estate was taking ages to arrive. They talked about phones, PlayStation versus Xbox and their boxing heroes. Horse pulled Marcus to one side. 'What's all this about a hearing test?' he asked Marcus.

The question caught Marcus by surprise. 'Who told you that?'

'It's got around … is it serious?'

'Nah.' Marcus pulled out a hospital appointment card from his back pocket and showed it to Horse.

'It's next week, Tuesday afternoon,' said Horse, scrutinising the card, 'we've got geography mocks then.'

'Drats!' said Marcus, sarcastically, 'I'll just have to miss geography mocks then, won't I? Miss Podborsky will so miss me.'

'Hey Marcus, this hearing thing, I'm with you thick and thin. You get me?'

'Yeh,' said Marcus. 'It's probably nothing … I don't want to talk about it, though. Okay?'

'Sure,' said Horse. The two of them re-joined the others. The chat had moved on to grossest killer movies but there was still tension. Only one thing was really on their minds, Marcus knew, an itch they were all dying to scratch.

Leonard was the one who finally scratched it. 'That penalty, I can't understand. I did everything right,' he announced.

'Course you did,' Horse said. The others agreed, Marcus kept quiet.

'Look left, shoot right. Every time it worked. Every time. Till today.'

'It's just one of them things, Lenny,' said Horse.

'Even I don't blame you, bro, and it should have been my kick,' said Jamil, through his one good eye. Jamil's other eye had completely disappeared behind swelling. 'Next time I'm bringing boxing gloves!'

For once, Jamil didn't get a laugh.

'Only one thing changed,' said Leonard, his face set in a mask of annoyance.

Marcus could sense something brewing, something in the way Leonard had not looked at him, or spoken to him directly since the match ended. Not in the dressing room. Not on the walk to the bus stop. Not now. Not yet.

'What's that, Lenny?' said Horse.

'Who was there at that penalty practice night?'

'We all were,' said Horse, '… and the girl,' he added, as an afterthought.

'Yes the girl. The one … hid in the bushes watching us practice. Anthony Vialli's sister,' Leonard said, and he finally turned to Marcus. 'What's her name, Marcus?'

'Adele,' Marcus said quietly. 'What are you getting at?'

Leonard half turned so he was addressing not just Marcus, but everyone. 'You see her jumping up and down like a flea when they scored? See her all through the match, cheering Bowker on?'

'It's her brother isn't it? She's gonna do that,' said Marcus.

'Yeh, it's her brother,' said Leonard. 'She's gonna do that. Cheer him on, help him. Question is how else did she help him?'

'My head aches,' said Jamil. 'I think my eye socket's bust.'

'Spit it out, Leonard,' said Horse, 'or shut up.'

'It's obvious what happened,' said Leonard slowly, turning once again to face Marcus. 'She watched us practice penalties. She heard me. "Look left, shoot right." She's told her brother and he's told their keeper.'

'Didn't happen,' Marcus said.

'How do you know?'

The two of them were close now. Within punching distance.

'You don't get it, do you, Marcus?' Leonard said, squaring up. He snatched Marcus's ATC out of his hand and flung it away. 'Your girlfriend spied on us! Your girlfriend cost us the league!'

'If you want to fight, let's do it,' Marcus said, 'just say the word.' He moved chin to chin with Leonard.

'Romeo, you can't be going out with her,' said Leonard, right in his face so Marcus could taste his breath.

Horse pushed between them. 'Cool it, Marcus. C'mon, Leonard. What's done is done, let it go.'

'My eye hurts like hell,' Jamil called out.

Leonard backed off. He walked back towards the bus stop bench and sat. Horse eased back to the bench himself and bounced Marcus's ATC over to him. Marcus trapped it under his foot first time.

'I don't want to fight you, Marcus,' said Leonard. He sounded tired. 'I'm just saying what's right for the team. There's only the Cup to play for now. It's our last chance.'

'I'm not going out with her,' said Marcus, flicking the ball up into his hands, 'we just meet up.' He felt awful saying it. He'd betrayed her.

'Whatever. But you can't be "seeing" her.' Leonard rolled his eyes for everyone's benefit, 'and hanging out with us.' Leonard looked around for support.

'That's bull,' Marcus said.

'I dunno,' Horse said. 'The Cup final's our last chance.'

Horse's reaction caught Marcus by surprise. Before he could respond, Horse said, 'that's your phone, Marky – your phone's ringing.'

'Right,' said Marcus, reaching to his pocket. He'd thought it was on vibrate.

Marcus looked down at his phone. Adele.

'Well? What's it to be then?' Leonard pressed. 'Her or us?'

'Give him time,' Horse said.

'No, it's cool,' said Marcus, turning on his heels. He could feel the pin pricks of tears stabbing his eyelids. He hated his eye ducts, how weak they were.

'Hey, Marcus!' Horse called.

But it was too late, Marcus was already gone.

THE SPY WHO LOVED ME

Marcus ran into the wind and rain. He didn't know if it was possible to feel any lower than he did. He felt like an old punch bag that was getting hit again and again by a queue of enraged people. Everything was his fault. Even Horse had deserted him.

He knew Leonard's game. For two long years Leonard had been forced to watch from the touchline as Marcus ran the team. Now that Marcus was out of the first-eleven, Leonard had finally seen his chance and was grabbing it with both hands. Sweet-talking tactics with Mr Davies, taking the kit home to be washed, organising the evening training sessions. Even buying everyone chips afterwards 'to replace the carbohydrates, since the chippy doesn't do energy drinks!' Everyone loved Leonard now. He'd made it into the team and he was sucking up to one and all to make sure he stayed in it.

He should have popped Leonard good and hard at the bus stop, Marcus thought. That would have been great, seeing Leonard's busted nose spurting blood.

He kept running. Soon he was soaked in sweat and rain. His arms and legs ached so much they screamed to stop but he kept on. His tears mingled with sweat and the soak of rain on his face.

Suddenly he felt his phone vibrate. He stopped and looked at the blue screen. Adele again. He answered it. She asked what was wrong with his breathing. He said he was fine, he'd been running. She wanted to meet him outside Westfield swimming pool. He told her, 'fine, ten minutes'.

The wind had stopped. His ATC was underneath his foot. He hadn't remembered kicking it while he'd been running. He scooped it up. He was keen to see Adele but she had caused him so much grief by turning up at the training session. And this doubt lingered in his mind, no matter how much he publicly denied it, no matter how hard he tried to dismiss it: What if she really was a spy?

Marcus stopped running at the top of the road where the swimming pool was. Why was he running to see her? Despite what he'd said to the team that day at training, she was not his girlfriend. Or was she? He thought maybe he should google 'girlfriend definition' and find out what it meant. He walked the last three hundred metres.

She was standing in the dome of white light cast by the building's security lamp, leaning against some giant yellow plastic pipes that were lying in the road. She waved when she saw him.

He leaned with her against the pipes.

'You okay?' She shot him a glance.

He flicked his ATC from foot to foot. 'Yeh. Why d'you say that?'

'I dunno.'

'And we didn't lose. We drew.'

'What do you mean?' said Adele.

'We lost the match but we were level on points but they had a higher goal difference.'

'Whatever,' Adele said. She covered his hand with hers. It startled him. Yet he left it there. Neither of them said anything for a moment.

'I'm sorry about …' Adele said finally.

Adele spoke so quietly Marcus couldn't make out what she said at the end of her sentence. 'You're sorry that I'm mad?' he asked quietly back.

'No, I'm sorry about my dad.'

'You mean …?'

'Yeh. What he shouted at the referee.'

Marcus remembered her dad jabbing at the referee and what he'd said. He couldn't make out why someone would say something like that. What did the referee's colour have to do with anything? But, like Horse said, racism wasn't logical. Some people got pleasure from throwing their weight around any which way they could. He could tell Mr Vialli was one of them. Eventually Adele nudged him. 'What are you thinking?'

'They're saying you're a spy again.'

Marcus was about to ask her if she'd known about the penalty tactic but, sitting with her now, the idea seemed daft again. So instead he said: 'They tried to ban me from seeing you. "You or them", they said.'

'And you chose me?' she laughed.

He hadn't thought of it like that. He watched how it amused her. Everything amused her.

'I'm suspended from the team anyway,' Marcus said, 'so it's same difference.'

Yet he knew he couldn't not see his mates. All he ever did in the evening was hang out with his bus stop crew. What else could he do? Disappear into his PlayStation? Watch TV with his mum if she wasn't out selling double-glazing, or with his dad if he wasn't whizzing

89

off to sing in some old pub? What kind of mates did he have, that did not take his word? They knew he lived for football and he'd never do anything to damage the team. Jamil knew that. Horse knew that. Ira knew that. It was Leonard who was the troublemaker.

'You're hurting my hand,' Adele said.

'Sorry.' Marcus hadn't realised he'd been holding her hand, let alone squeezing it. He let go of it. 'I bet your brother's having a party right now. And you were right. We wouldn't have lost if I'd been playing.'

Marcus didn't know why he said that last bit. He hadn't meant it boastfully.

'I know,' Adele said, 'my dad said as soon as they saw you weren't on the team, it was game, set and match.'

He looked across at her.

'My dad's warned me off you,' she said.

'How does he know?'

'Leonard told my-talented-brother in the middle of the pitch. He told Dad … so we're both now banned from seeing each other. Like Romeo and Juliet.'

Marcus said nothing.

'I'm cold,' Adele said, 'let's walk.'

They got off the pipes and walked. Neither of them spoke. The rain started again, a big dolloppy, splish-splashy rain that had most people running for doorways.

Adele told him her dad had got the Manchester United scout's phone number on speed dial. If Anthony got the apprenticeship at the club, their dad had said they'd be so rich, they'd be set up for life. Not just Anthony, the whole family would be sorted, which would be good because even though they looked rich, they needed the money. Her dad had told Adele that if it had been Anthony who was suspended from school, he would have been beating down the door of the headteacher to get his son back on the team and back in school. In that order. Marcus didn't say anything.

'How is Anthony about me and you?' he asked.

'He's annoyed, which is excellent.'

'What did you tell him?'

'What do you think?'

'Why do you always answer a question with a question?'

'I told him we were going to run away and get married.'

'You're joking?'

'That's what he said. Then I said we're just friends and you were helping me with my maths. Which is true, right? Explain to me again what a quadrilateral equation is. The bit after the square root bit.'

'You really want to know?'

'Not really. I just like the sound of your voice when you say it. You get so into it, like you're *in love* with the quadrilateral!'

Marcus spent the rest of the early evening with Adele walking and talking in the stop-start rain. He enjoyed it but he never lost the sour taste in his mouth that had come with losing the league decider. And something troubled him. The way Adele had laughed about him being forced to choose between his mates and her, as if it had no meaning, perhaps it didn't to her. Or perhaps she was a spy? He wanted it not to be true, every cell in his body willed it to be not true. Yet he couldn't be sure.

WHAT LOSING FEELS LIKE

Monday at school was strange. In form-class, Jamil cold-shouldered him. Marcus didn't mind. Jamil was like that sometimes. He had a black eye-patch on and spent most of his time in class walking up and down ooh-arring with it. Marcus didn't need a clown as a friend. At break he hung by the stairs and played text tennis with Adele.

Everybody h8s me @ skul 2day.

H8rs gotta h8. tell them to go xxxx themslfs

Tick

Nix dat. think it but don't say it - i did that myslf n got report card. Was BORING.

2 l8 I jus sed it.

Lol

Nobody heard me tho. am in corridor.

Send me a pic

Marcus sent her a selfie.

Am likin da snarl n cute tach. U luk like a grime star

Tnx

Soz agen abt my dad

Gotta go. No credit left c ya

He didn't want to talk about Adele's dad. It was strange, but he felt angrier about it now than when he first heard it. Everyone was talking about it, the whole school, especially the black kids. They wanted to do something about it but nobody had thought of anything yet.

Marcus was right under one of the school bells and heard it ring loud and clear. It was his year group assembly day. They were going to be told about their subject options, what they could choose, and when. All of Year 9 trooped into the hall, class by class, nine classes in all. Ozone, the head of year gave a long speech about destiny. Then he said Mr Davies was going to talk about the football team's 'amazing achievements'. Ozone sounded sarcastic. Mr Davies came to the front of the hall. He seemed sadder than usual, and nervous in a shiny grey suit.

'Thank you for that introduction, Mr Wrexham,' Mr Davies began. The other teachers were looking bored already. The science teacher began playing with his Blackberry, and Ozone was having a whisper with a languages teacher.

'I'm not going to do some crime scene autopsy on the dead body of our chances,' Mr Davies said in a jokey tone. He pointed upwards. 'The sun is out … and it's going to shine on us. We can still reach for the stars, however high the sky. Hope can still swell our hearts. This is not the beginning of the end just the end … the beginning. We came second … the league. That means we beat nine out of ten other teams. And we can win the cup final!'

There was silence. Then a girl in the back row giggled. Mr Davies glared her into silence.

It was funny how popularity worked, Marcus thought as Mr Davies stumbled on. When Marcus had been the star of the school football team, everyone wanted to sit at his table at lunch, walk with him from class to class, play football with him at break. The lower year groups even wanted to carry his bag. Now, not two weeks had gone by since he was suspended from the team and he was playing keepy-uppy on his own at break and everyone was hanging out with Leonard.

'The journey of a thousand miles …' Mr Davies continued. It sounded like he'd swallowed a book of Hollywood phrases.

Marcus wondered if this popularity thing was the same with teachers. Before the team lost the league, Mr Davies had sat mid-table in the teacher's league, above the art and cookery teachers, below the English and maths departments. Now he had dropped into the relegation zone with careers and non-English-speaking new arrivals. Mr Davies didn't deserve that. They could have won. The head of year should not have listened to Miss Podborsky. Geography was the first subject Marcus was dropping.

After, in the scrum of bodies fleeing the assembly, Leonard popped Marcus's ATC out from under his arm. He claimed it was accidental, but Marcus knew better. Marcus slammed him into a wall and threw a punch. He missed, but the ache in his knuckle where he hit the noticeboard felt good. As did the flash of fear in Leonard's eyes and how everyone jumped back. Leonard tried to knee him in the groin. He pushed an elbow into Leonard's neck and held it there. Leonard punched away at his ribs. There was a whole bunch of people around them.

'What's up with you two?' Horse asked, pulling them apart.

'Him and his stupid girlfriend spy!' Leonard said, looking round for support. 'He lost us the match!'

Horse sighed. 'This again? We're already late for double maths. Everyone, before dinner, meet behind the labs.'

Behind the labs was the one place the school's CCTV didn't cover.

'Agreed? Or do I have to bust heads?'

When Horse talked like that, no one argued. Maths couldn't end too soon.

Behind the labs, Leonard was waiting. He had most of the team around him. As Marcus walked up, they all looked away, or glared. Leonard said something in his direction. Everybody sniggered.

'What was that?' said Marcus.

'Eh? Eh? Eh?' mocked Leonard, cupping his hand to an ear.

'Let's do this then,' Horse said, 'finish it.'

Marcus braced himself. But instead of rushing at him, Leonard worked his tongue again, taking up straight where he had left off. 'He lost us the league. And he'll lose us the Cup final if we talk to him. His girlfriend will find out our tactics and tell her brother!'

'Maybe you just took a rubbish penalty, Lenny?' Marcus said. It was the one thing nobody had dared say, but Marcus was sick of nobody saying it. He watched it strike home. For one beautiful moment, Leonard's face was a picture of embarrassment, shock and fear all mashed together. And in that moment everyone could see that there had to be some truth in what Marcus had just said.

Then Leonard flew at him. Marcus was ready. He ducked and thumped Leonard hard in the stomach as Leonard swung high. Leonard dropped to one knee, but got up again and charged, head first. Marcus sidestepped, and kicked Leonard's back. Leonard collapsed. Horse stepped over him to protect him. 'That's enough!' said Horse.

The rest of the team joined Horse helping Leonard up. Horse dusted himself down, cursing under his breath. His shirt was ripped at the collar. 'Anybody got anything else to say?' was all Horse said, when it was all calmed down.

Marcus saw Leonard had a busted lip. It felt good. Leonard the Lip silenced. He couldn't help smirking.

'Anyone?' said Horse again. It sounded like a threat.

There was a general shuffle of feet. The labs were close to the canteen and cooking smells were wafting over.

'Right,' said Horse. 'We lost because Marcus wasn't playing. Simple as. If Mr Davies comes up with new tactics we'll keep them under wraps, for what they're worth. That includes Marcus. Got it, Marcus?'

Marcus nodded.

'We're done then,' said Horse, reaching for his bag. 'End of. Let's go. I'm starving. That's the last dinner bell.'

Everyone raced to get to the canteen before the dinner ladies drew the shutters down on the food trays. They made it just in time. Marcus sat alone. Jamil and Horse sat with Leonard. Leonard's lips both the clean one and the busted one, were working overtime. Marcus could see them, heads down, listening to Leonard, even as they ate. Leonard was never going to give up.

Later, Mr Davies was in a better mood at football practice after school than he had been at assembly. He gathered them all into one penalty area.

'Afternoon boys. Listen, I'm sorry you had to hear what one of the Bowker parents said. That … a racial abuse and it shouldn't be flipping happening. I was appalled and I've written the league a stern letter.'

'That will sort it!' someone called out sarcastically.

'Give him a break,' someone else said.

'Yes, give me a break, heaven knows I need one,' Mr Davies said.

Everyone remembered how he'd been treated at assembly by the other staff and quietly understood. Things settled down.

'I made notes on the Bowker players,' the coach continued. 'We can take them. It means do… things different in midfield and working … forward line around to attack their weaknesses in defence. They won't know what's hit them. Right, set out the cones!'

The warm-up routines started. Marcus threw himself into it. He was two-thirds of the way through his attack of the line of cones when he heard Mr Davies shouting his name. 'Marky! Marky! Come here!'

Marcus trotted over.

'You've got cloth ears, haven't you, lad?' Mr Davies scolded him, even as he wrapped an arm around him. 'I said left foot slalom, not right foot slalom. You're a bit of a dreamer, Marky aren't you?'

Marcus said nothing but steadied himself. The tell-tale twitch on Mr Davies forehead told Marcus he was going to launch into an anecdote, and once Mr Davies started an anecdote, he never stopped till he got to the end so you had to just roll with it.

'Concentration means knowing not only where the ball is, but where every other player on the pitch is,' Mr Davies duly began. 'There was a great Man United player called Eric Cantona and he always knew where his teammates were, like he had a 360 degree radar on the top of his head. You gave him the ball and – bam – it was either in the net or at the feet of one of his team mates. Why? Concentration. Awareness. All the great players had it. Otherwise you're just a show pony, lots …'

Marcus had this stray thought. That it was funny how, when you didn't hear something, people found a way of blaming you. He knew it wasn't his fault. He was used to it by now though.

He continued to listen to Mr Davies '… tricks but no use to your team. Cristiano Ronaldo was a show pony when he joined Man United. By the time they sold him to Real Madrid he'd learned to concentrate. Real Madrid did not pay eighty-million for a show pony, Marcus. Concentrate. Left foot slalom, off you go.'

Everyone else had done the routine and they were all standing around. Marcus sped towards the cones with his training ball and nailed the left foot slalom first time, inch perfect, every cone. They clapped.

'Brilliant!' shouted Mr Davies. 'And that's what we're looking for, close ball skills. It makes the difference: in a tight match, who has the skills, wins. Now two teams. Team one: Jamil, Horse, Leonard, Ira, Dinners. Team two: Busta, Level One, Shaun, Mikey, Rowan. Marcus, over here by me.'

Marcus immediately picked up that team one was the midfield Mr Davies had chosen for the Cup final. The fact Marcus was not in either team hit him hard. What was he even doing in his kit? He stood with Mr Davies, as the five-a-side session got going.

'Lose the long face, Marcus,' chided Mr Davies, 'and stop fiddling with your phone. Yes, you're on the sidelines for the final, but use it to your advantage. It's an opportunity to watch how we play for next year.

Concentrate. See how Horse always drifts wide, but Ira plugs the gap. See how Ira's back-pedalling soon as they lose the ball? Superb. You catch how Jamil shifted it from left foot to right? He doesn't like it on his left, remember that. He's flying with it now. See the hole their centre-backs have left because Jamil has dragged his marker one way, and Horse has gone the other? A huge gap. Watch. See. Learn. 360 degree vision, that's the modern game. Leonard in the hole! Leonard! Stop, lads! Stop! stop!'

The game stopped and Mr Davies pointed out the problem. 'Leonard, you've got to bang it in the zone, not where he is, but where he will be. There was a huge gap there. Try land it on the exact spot you pick out, it's like a dart board and the ball's the arrow, land it bull's eye. Try it again. Positions!'

Team one did the same routine. Horse left, Jamil right. Leonard's final pass missed the mark again. It was a tricky one for Leonard, Marcus guessed, a thirty metre flight into the gap.

'C'mon, Leonard,' said Mr Davies, getting exasperated. 'It's all there. We just need that final pass.'

Leonard got upset. 'You do it!' he said to Mr Davies, kicking the ball over. Mr Davies trapped it under his feet at the third attempt.

Everyone knew that Mr Davies, though an okay coach, was rubbish at actually playing football. There was a moment while Mr Davies squirmed. Finally he said, 'I can't do it, Leonard, you know that.'

Marcus felt sorry for the coach. 'Give me the ball,' Marcus said, 'I'll do it.'

The coach rolled the ball over to Marcus. Marcus moved into Leonard's midfield position. The teams got ready.

'Okay, go!' Mr Davies shouted.

Jamil ran, Horse made his run in the opposite direction. The ball came to Marcus. He flighted it and it landed dead at Jamil's rushing feet. Jamil smacked it with his right foot between the goalpost cones and did a crazy celebratory jig. Everyone laughed.

'See? Leonard, your turn,' called Mr Davies. 'Marcus, knock him the ball!'

'It's windy,' complained Leonard.

'Okay. Marcus. Do it again!' commanded Mr Davies.

There was a light wind blowing now. Jamil and Horse made the same moves, dragging the defenders out of position. Marcus drilled the ball, same spot, but with slightly more power to compensate for the wind. It touched down within a half metre of Jamil and Jamil finished it off again. He did the same whoops and arms-high, knee-high celebration.

'See? Have a go, Leonard,' said Mr Davies.

Marcus knocked the ball over to Leonard. Reluctantly, Leonard stepped into position. All eyes were on him. Jamil and Horse did their runs. Leonard walloped the ball. It flew up too high, and five metres beyond Jamil.

'Again,' said Mr Davies.

Leonard stepped up again. His mouth, bruised lip and all, was screwed up with determination. Leonard's second attempt was no better than the first. His head dropped. Someone kicked the ball towards Leonard for him to have a third attempt but Leonard had turned his back on the ball and it rolled past him. Marcus trapped it and dribbled it up to Leonard. As he placed the ball at Leonard's feet, Marcus nudged him. Leonard looked up. His eyes were fierce and sad. He was being humiliated. Marcus knew what Leonard was doing wrong. All he needed to tell him was, 'lean over it more, Leonard, and it'll stay down'. Leonard stared at him. His eyes begged Marcus to help. Marcus weakened. But then, he thought, why should he help him after all that Leonard had said and done to him?

'Again Leonard!' shouted Mr Davies. 'We're going to do this till we get it right!'

Marcus retreated to the sidelines.

'Okay, go!' cried Mr Davies.

Jamil and Horse shot into position. Leonard hit the ball, this time he leaned even further back. The ball drilled through to Jamil but way high. Jamil leaped to take it on his head, but even Jamil couldn't make the height.

This was useless, Marcus thought. He turned away, bored. Something else was on his mind and had been on his mind for a long time. He got out his phone and wandered away from the pitch.

Dwayne and Mohammad, the two BowkerVale players who had hung out with Marcus during summer school were in his contacts list. The two of them had to have felt it when Mr Vialli had called the ref a black bastard. They were black too. He texted them both.

'Blk Bstd'? Yr new coach gon 2 far dudes. It got 2 b sorted by ne means nec. Nuh?-Marcus

Few things were bigger than football, Marcus thought, but this was one. He just managed to finish the text when the coach came calling him. 'Marcus, you're needed!'

He looked over. Leonard was in a sulk and the other players had their heads hanging. Leonard still couldn't flight a simple ball.

'I can't teach him,' Marcus said, 'I don't know how, I just do it.'

'I know you better than that, Marky,' said Mr Davies, walking with him over to the ball. 'Show him how, like in slo-mo.' Mr Davies did a slow-motion action of a man running to strike a ball. It got him laughs. Marcus smiled but shrugged.

'Do it!' Horse said, approaching him. Horse's brow plunged, like he was going to drop Marcus there and then if Marcus didn't do as asked.

'Why should I do anything for him? Eh? Eh? Eh?' Marcus said to Horse. Now who's amused, Marcus thought.

'Don't push me, Marcus,' said Horse.

'Alright boys, easy now,' said Mr Davies. 'Are you going to show him or not, Marky? Go on, lad, just once.'

Reluctantly, Marcus planted the ball down on the free kick spot. Everyone got in position. Mr Davies waved play. Marcus skied the ball. There were groans all round.

'I don't know,' said Marcus, 'the moment I think about it I can't do it.'

'I'm disappointed in you,' said the coach. 'Not angry. Disappointed. I thought you were better than this pettiness.'

Marcus shrugged. Yes, he'd deliberately skied it. But he didn't feel bad at all. Maybe it would teach Leonard something.

Leonard tried again. By his tenth effort he was getting it in the zone at least. Finally Jamil managed to pluck one out of the sky. He let it drop, took it at half-volley and smashed it home, then did his jig. A desperately relieved Leonard joined in with him.

'There you go boys,' said Mr Davies, 'that's what it's about. Never give up. And again!'

Half an hour later, as they trooped back to the changing room, Leonard had made all of three good passes, but the coach was happy and was making out like Leonard had it all nailed now and they had every chance of winning.

When they got to the changing room, Mr Davies went off to deal with the broken-down water heater.

'This Cup final's gonna be Ghana versus Germany!' Jamil shouted excitedly above the general racket.

'What are you talking about … Sparrow?' someone jeered back. Jamil had his eye patch back on and looked like a pirate again. 'Jack' was the word that had been said before 'Sparrow', Marcus worked out.

'Simple. It's Black versus White. Our team's black, Bowker's is white!' Jamil declared.

'So I'm black am I?' said Dinners, the centre-back. He was white, with orange freckles.

'You can't talk Bowker white can you?' said Jamil. 'Oh excuse me chaps, what a good game', Jamil imitated a posh accent.

'Nope,' said Dinners.

'And would you have said what that Bowker captain's dad said?' Jamil quizzed him.

'Hell no!' replied Dinners.

'Then you, my friend, are a brother, you are black, bro!'

Everyone cheered and Jamil duly conferred honorary black player status on all three of the white players in the changing room. Ghana v Germany stuck in the team's imagination and the shout of 'Ghana! Ghana!' rang round the dressing room, even though, Marcus reflected, neither team was all white or all black. The Ducie team was *mostly* black and the Bowker team was *mostly* white. But no-one cared for that distinction. Ideas were funny like that Marcus thought, they stuck, independently of the truth. Ideas just had to feel right to a group of people and that was that. Like the idea that Leonard could replace him.

Marcus began unlacing his boots as the general din rose. What was 'black', anyway, he thought. They had done a family tree exercise in Year 8, and, of the players he knew for sure, Horse was a quarter Jamaican, a quarter Guadeloupian, a quarter Turkish and a quarter English. Jamil was half Jamaican, a quarter Nigerian, and a quarter Polish. Andrew was half Ghanaian, half Scottish-English. Sanjay's parents were from Uganda and India, and Ira was a hundred per cent Jamaican though his family were all light skinned and looked Indian. It was more like the United Nations v Germany, than Ghana v Germany, but Marcus kept that thought to himself. What was flavour of the month was what won the day, not necessarily what was true.

Jamil was in fine form in the changing room. He got the conversation going about what Mr Vialli had said. Everyone on the pitch and everyone on the touchline had heard it. Jamil said the referee had rung the authorities and it had become a 'racial incident' and Mr Vialli had been told to write a personal letter of apology to the referee. Jamil called for a vote on whether Mr Vialli should be banned from the touchline. It was carried unanimously.

Mr Davies made it back. The showers were off and they'd have to head out as they were, he explained. Nobody minded that much; everyone knew the school didn't have the money to fix the showers properly so they broke down every month.

As Marcus walked home on his own, the weight of being out of the school team had him dragging his feet. Going to the training sessions was like getting ready for a party that you knew you were going to be turned away from. The new tactics might work. If they could drag Bowker's centre-backs out of position and drop the ball into the gap for Jamil to run onto. They had spent most of the practice session on it and they knew what they had to do. They had worked on some neat set pieces too, working out when to play long, when to play short and what the options were and how the dead ball kicker – Leonard – would signal what he was going to do: left hand high meant long ball. Right hand high meant short ball.

Marcus knew he would be out tonight on the pitch practicing shimmies, left-right ball switches, knee traps and dead ball kicks. Practice. Practice. Practice. Yet what point was that practice when he was banned from the team? He'd be a spectator at the Cup final. He might have lost his only chance of being in a final. And the Man United scout would be there for sure, watching Anthony, not him; and possibly Leonard. That would be the pits, if Leonard got the glory and the agent's signature.

Somebody slapped Marcus's head. Marcus balled up his fists, thinking it was Leonard. He was about to fling a punch when he saw who it actually was.

Horse.

Going past at a trot. Horse turned, so he was jogging backwards.

'Caught you there,' Horse said. 'You didn't hear me shouting?'

Marcus shook his head.

'Anyway, don't be such a … at training next time!'

Marcus couldn't make out what the '…' was but he could guess. Horse had never slapped him like that before. His head still hurt. He watched Horse disappear.

Had he been out of order not to show Leonard how to drill a ball? If it had been anybody else he would have, but not Leonard. His whole body tensed even at the thought of the name. *Leonard.* Marcus turned the name round in his mind, trying to weaken its spell. Leonard the Lip. Leonard the Loser. Lemony Leonard. Leonard had made fun of him. He had wrecked his shin. He had taken his place on the team. Why in a hundred years should he help him?

Of course Horse never let the team down. He'd once been hospitalised clearing a ball in a goalmouth scramble. He'd whacked the ball off the goal line but run into a goalpost. Next day at school Horse had shrugged it off and only wanted to know if they'd won. The team was everything for Horse. Maybe Horse was right and he should think only of the team, even if that meant helping Leonard. It rankled too much though. And Marcus simply couldn't bring himself to do it. Not after what Leonard had put him through.

That evening on the pitch, Marcus practiced like never before. He was still vexed with Leonard and now with Horse as well. He did half his routines but felt feverish and decided to sit on the wall for a minute.

All around him people on the estate were busy doing their things: fixing cars, taking in washing, smacking golf balls around the park, yammering into mobile phones as they walked along. Dogs roamed across the park in packs the way the dogs of Westfield did. The familiarity of everything calmed him. He got his energy back.

He practiced dead ball kicks. He struck the ball on the left side so it span left, then had it spinning right and finally (it was the hardest thing to do) span it on its horizontal axis – so it rotated forwards as it travelled. The forward spin was the Holy Grail of spins. It made the ball balloon up, but then dip viciously and suddenly as it neared the goal. It was almost impossible to pull off. Only the great Cristiano Ronaldo could do it every time. Marcus managed it once in thirty attempts that evening, but he was content with that. It was one more than he had ever achieved before.

Instead of going home, he phoned his mum and said he was going to grab a bag of chips then do his homework with a mate. His mum moaned but had to let him.

ADELE AND THE
MARSEILLE ROULETTE

Marcus slid past the Hawaiian pub. Smokers were standing outside nursing their cigarettes and pints. His dad had sung there every Saturday years ago and some of the regulars still recognised him from when his dad had taken him along. Adele was waiting for him by the pipes outside the swimming pool. He slumped next to her. She was looking up into the sky when he arrived.

'See that bird hanging there without even moving its wings?' she asked.

'It's thermals,' Marcus said, 'a current of—'

'I know what thermals is, I'm not thick you know,' she glared at him.

'What maths do you need to practice?' Marcus said, thinking, he should have spotted Adele was in a mood, she had her bottom lip pushed out and her arms crossed around herself.

'Geometry.'

He quizzed her on basic formulas as he juggled his ATC. She got most of them right.

He asked her why she didn't like doing her homework at home.

'No-one's ever there to help,' Adele replied. 'Dad lives in his office. Mum's a zombie. You could set the house on fire and she wouldn't notice.'

'What's your mum depressed about?'

Adele shrugged. 'Me? "What do you want to do with your life? What subjects are you choosing? Are they suitable? Are you going to University? Don't sit with your legs like that, it's not ladylike! Don't pick your nose! Where are you going? You can't wander round town on your own!"'

'Um.'

'It's never Anthony. He can get away with anything. Why? "Because he's a boy!"'

'Um.' Marcus was trying Zidane's signature Marseille Roulette: the double step on, then spin out.

'This morning she sits in the bathroom looking at her face, saying she's getting old. I tell her, "you're not getting old, you are old, silly cow!" She bursts into tears. Total waterfall. I give her a kiss, say I'm sorry, and she's not really old, just old-ish, and we sit there putting each other's make up on. And she's happy and hugs me like she's trying to squeeze toothpaste out of me. Next thing I know she's … out on her bed.'

'Um.'

'Say "um" again and you're toast.'

'What? Oh. How's your brother?'

'He told Dad off about what he said to the referee. They had a blazing row, you should have heard it.' She imitated Anthony's voice. '"You make me sick, how could you say something like that, you could of got the whole team banned!"'

'Your Anthony wouldn't lend me money for a sandwich at summer school,' Marcus said, still trying and failing with the Zidane move.

'Yeh, well, my brother takes after his dad. Don't be fooled by his nicey nicey talk. I can't stand either of them.'

Marcus did a flick and cradled the ball between his shoulders while still looking at Adele.

'My dad would so not like this,' said Adele, watching him for once.

'Because?'

'Duh. Because you're black.'

'I'm not going out with your dad though, am I? I'm going out with you,' Marcus said.

'If we was going out,' Adele corrected him.

'Yeh, yeh, that's what I meant. Anyway, I can't talk tactics with you.'

'Uh, tell me then Marky,' Adele, said, in her spy voice, 'you're gonna start with 4 4 3, then at half-time switch to 6 3 1, but if you go a goal down its 15 1 and bring on an elephant?'

'No comment,' Marcus replied.

'Where did you get your hair …?'

'What do you mean, where did I get my hair? I was born with it.'

Adele laughed. 'No, I said, "where did you get your hair *cut*?"'

'Oh. At Mustapha's by the indoor market.' Actually Marcus's mum had cut his hair, but Marcus would rather die than say that.

Adele got going on a list of things boys thought girls liked but that she didn't. Marcus tried following it for a while, but Adele was talking into her hands and he didn't hear bits of it and anyway he lost interest. He wanted to nail the Zidane move.

'Hey, Marky, I'm over here, are you listening?' said Adele.

'Course,' Marcus said.

'I'm bored. Let's go to the petrol station.'

'We got no money,' said Marcus.

'Who needs money?' winked Adele.

'You're crazy,' Marcus said.

'I want some excitement.'

Marcus leaned over and pressed his lips to her cheek, quickly. Then he jumped off the pipes.

'Was that a kiss?' she asked.

'Yes.' Marcus flicked his ATC up in the air, thinking, what had come over him? Why had he kissed her? He felt dizzy.

'Now I'm even more bored,' was all she said.

They walked to the bus station. It was a long glass shed surrounded by bus lanes, with boarded up shops to one side and an empty parking lot to the other. It looked like a scene from a horror movie, before the mad killer struck. All it needed was an eerie soundtrack.

'You can't wait here,' Marcus said.

'I always wait here. They've got CCTV. Look.'

Twin black pylons towered above the station. 'It covers everywhere,' she said.

'Fine. Still I'll wait with you. Got nothing else to do.'

'Suit yourself.'

Adele sat on one of the plastic fold-down seat panels. Marcus began doing tricks.

'BORING!' she called out, but he carried on anyway.

Out of nowhere a small crowd gathered. Even the CCTV camera swung round. Marcus stepped it up. He enjoyed the crowds, though he tried his hardest tricks, like the Marseille Roulette, only when there was no one around.

The station tannoy speaker squawked, catching Marcus by surprise. He almost dropped the ball. He saved it with a leaping scorpion kick that drew a smattering of applause.

'What'd it say?' Marcus called to Adele.

'"Members of the public are reminded there is no ball playing at this station!"' Adele told him, in a nasal squeak that imitated the tannoy. Then she gave the CCTV camera the finger. At that moment, her bus swung into the station. With a quick wave, she dived into the crowd that piled into the bus's open doors. Marcus ran up and tapped the window where she sat. She blew him a kiss. The bus pulled away. Suddenly, the bus station was just a bus station.

Walking home, Marcus thought about Adele. She had the ideal family. Yet the way she described it, her family was worse than his. He thought about her dad and what he'd said, 'black bastard'. Two of Bowker Vale's own team were black and their goalkeeper was Chinese. Hadn't Mr Vialli seen that before he'd opened his gob? Bowker Vale's Dwayne had texted back to his text with an '*ok bro*'. He didn't know what it meant, he could only guess. His thoughts drifted around. The referee sending Mr Vialli off was brilliant. If only Marcus could send off everyone who gave him a hard time. Miss Podborsky? Red Card! Mr Head of Year? Red Card!

Adele. He always came back to thinking about her. He liked the story she told about swapping tomato ketchup for chilli sauce then watching her brother gasp when he splodged it all over his chips and began scoffing them. He liked the way her lower lip dropped and rolled outward a little when she was thinking about something. He liked what she did when he tried to explain for the fifth time the difference between modes, means and medians. She'd drop her bottom lip and go squint-eyed.

Marcus turned the key in his front door and stepped inside. His mum wasn't downstairs but his dad was on the sofa. The TV was blaring so he switched it off. He could see his dad's tonsils in the back of his mouth, two pink balls vibrating in a Newton's cradle of snores. His dad shifted in his sleep and farted. He had the picture of Marcus's granddad – the one that was usually on the wall – on his chest. It rested there precariously. One turn and it was gone. Dads were overrated, Marcus decided as he carefully took the photo off his dad without waking him and placed it back on the wall.

He went into the kitchen and made a jam butty then came back out, nudged his dad's legs and squeezed himself onto the sofa. Up close, his dad's snore was a cross between a bus engine on idle, and somebody dragging a dead body across a gravel track. His face was pock-marked from the acne he had suffered when he was Marcus's age. Marcus felt a tingling in the centre of his own forehead. Sometimes he felt jinxed. He consoled himself with another jam butty. Then he went upstairs, lay on his bed a while. Something in his gut made him restless. He got up, went to his window and texted Adele.

U bak ok?
Sure.
Stil cant believ we lost

Soz (The 'soz' came with a photo of Adele doing her saddest face).

Becos of penalties

Even worse. Send me a pic

He sent her a selfie

Nice bedrum posters. U luk bad what hapd 2 your hair? It all mushed.

Was lyin in bed we lost gess its not the end ov da world.

Best chek tho? Luk out yr window! (This came with a pic of Adele with her hair all flicked up and wild eyed horror stare)

Marcus laughed.

C ya

PASS THE KETCHUP

Mum yelled, 'Come get your tea, Marky!' He came down. The hearing test letter was on his mind but he wasn't sure anyone wanted to listen. He sat at the table with his mum, dad and sister and tucked into the spaghetti bolognese. As usual, nobody actually talked to anyone else at the table.

'I'm not getting any decent leads,' Mum was saying to no-one in particular. 'If I got decent leads … They're giving me the old lists. The stiffs. The Moveds. The Refused-Credits. And the call centre goons are promising fifty per cent discount. I have to double the start price to cover that. I'm slipping down the chart … Maybe I should go blonde, maybe that would work better on the doorsteps, what do you think, J?'

'I think Leah might have the singing talent,' said Dad. 'She takes after her dad. She was singing in her bath this morning. She was so happy. I'm feeling lucky today, gonna buy a lottery ticket.'

Mum kept on with her own monologue. 'My boss you know, she can kiss me where-the-sun-don't-shine. Reason I'm sinking down that chart is cos she gives me duff leads. Last week it was a caravan site. Would you believe? A caravan site? To sell double glazing? I phoned and told her right off, heads will roll, wasting my time. She blamed a postcode mix-up, said try them anyway, they might have friends with houses, could be holiday homes. Ridiculous. Meanwhile Derek got the housing association pitch. I mean Derek? I won't diss him but that mumbler? Pitching for four thousand windows and a three year maintenance contract? My God, you know something's going on between them. If he's getting that pitch, the broom cupboard's been busy. I've had enough, I'm working on my vanishing act. Then kazoom! I'm gone. And I'm keeping the laptop. They owe it me, the amount of unpaid overtime I'm putting in. It's the least they owe me. Who wants more spaghetti?'

'Does anyone want to know what I did today?' Marcus said.

'You did go to school, right?' probed Mum.

'Gaga dadodadagoo!' said Leah.

'Did you hear that? She just said Dada!' said Dad. 'That's because I'm spending all my time looking after her while others traipse around caravan parks on hopeless double glazing calls. She knows who does the looking after in this house. Say it again, cutie. "Dada. Dada."'

'Gagadoda dodagoo!' said Leah.

'There's a clever girl!'

'Oh, beam me up, Scottie,' said Mum.

Marcus gave up on his parents. He turned to Leah. 'I'm going to tell you what I did today, Leah,' he said. Leah gave him a rice pudding smile.

'What I did was—'

'Marcus eat your dinner before it gets cold. I'm expecting Bones,' said Dad.

Marcus groaned. Bones was Dad's mate. If Bones sat with them, Marcus would get up and leave and his dad knew it. All Bones ever spoke about was how much money there was in loading his wagon with butchers' scrap bones. When he visited their house the stench of rotting bones didn't leave for weeks.

'The baby will be asleep soon,' said Mum, 'I might try some leafleting.'

'What's up?' said Dad.

'Nothing,' said Marcus.

'You are worthy, son. You are related to an African Chief. We are not council estate trash. We are royalty. Pass the ketchup.'

THE SOUND BOOTH

It was the morning of his hearing test. He got into his uniform, grabbed a bowl of cereal and tried to sneak away. His mum blocked his way at the front door.

'Marcus, it's your hospital appointment isn't it, for your ears? I'm coming with you.'

'How did you know?'

'Doesn't matter.'

'You searched my room,' Marcus snapped. 'You're not coming.'

His mum looked at him and shuddered. 'I know you're a big boy now,' she said, 'but I'm your mother and I can't bear not to be there with you.'

'No.'

'It says on the letter you have to take an adult.'

'Move out of the way, Mum. You're. Not. Coming.'

'You can't do this to me, you can't be so cruel. I'm your mother!'

Her breathing was getting jerky again, like she might have an asthma attack. Marcus relented and immediately felt frustrated: Why did his mum always get her way?

'Alright, you can come but you're saying nothing. Not a word.'

'But—'

'Ah!'

'Fine. From now till when we get back, I'll say nothing.'

Marcus headed out, with his mum shadowing him four paces behind like a bad detective film.

He trudged on, remembering. When the appointment letter had come through the door, Mum had asked what the letter said. He told her it was none of her business. She was always saying she was too busy with the double glazing so why should he bother telling her? Yes. Some things you just had to do alone. As for Dad, he was always on shift-work.

Marcus found himself on the hospital bus, though he could not remember boarding it. He sat upstairs, making his mum follow him there even though she liked to ride on the lower deck. Somewhere in his mind he thought maybe there was something not quite right with his ears, but he was sure it was wax. His stomach was flipping.

The appointment was at 9.20 am and would last no more than half an hour, the letter said. He wondered how he would be feeling at 9.50 am. He realised he didn't have his ATC on him for the first time since he could remember. It felt weird, like there was a big hole under his arm.

He pressed the bell on the bus to get off at the hospital stop. A crowd of people got off with him, his mum pushing through them, trying to keep up with him. The main entrance was boarded up and a sign there said 'Temp Entrance' with an arrow pointing to other signs. There were signs everywhere. One sign read, 'Those wishing to attend the Eye Clinic please turn left then take the path on the right to the green entrance doors.' It struck Marcus as a particularly stupid sign. How could blind people read it? Marcus's destination was Ear Nose and Throat. Eye Clinic did not include Ear Nose and Throat he was sure. Maybe Ear Nose and Throat was another hospital somewhere completely different.

He glanced at his watch. 9.15 am. Which way? His mum didn't know either else she would have tugged his sleeve by now. This was stupid. Why was he putting himself through it? He could leave, give his mum the slip, tell the school the hospital said he was okay, or could make up a letter and send that, scan a signature onto it and hand it in at school. All he had to do was speed up, he thought, there were so many hospital buildings all scattered about you could lose anyone within two minutes if you tried hard enough. He imagined himself running like his shoes were on fire, all the way out of the hospital grounds, his mum flailing her arms trying to keep up.

'Marky!'

Marcus looked up. It was Horse. Bouncing Marcus's ATC.

'What are you doing here?' Marcus said. 'How did you get my ATC?'

Horse passed him his ball. 'I called at your house and your dad said you'd left already, so I guessed. He said to take the ball for you and you've got to phone him straight away after.'

'Thanks for the ball.'

Horse nodded.

Marcus waited for Horse to leave. Horse just stood there.

'What?' Marcus said.

'I'm coming with you,' said Horse, not budging.

'I don't need you.'

'I'm your mate. That's what mates do.'

'You slapped me.'

'Sometimes people need slapping,' Horse said, with a big shrug then a quick glance at Marcus' mum, who was hovering, as usual, and hadn't liked the sound of Marcus getting slapped. Marcus was impressed. His mum had been true to her word. She hadn't spoken, even now.

Horse softened. 'This isn't easy for me, Marky. Everyone's mad at you.'

'Leave me then. Take off like the rest of them.'

'That's not gonna happen. I'm mad at you. But you're still my mate.'

Marcus shrugged.

'Hello, Mrs Adenuga,' Horse said to Marcus's mum politely. She was stood leaning on a lamp post. He hadn't batted an eyelid that she wasn't standing next to Marcus.

Marcus's mum nodded, keeping her oath of silence.

They started off again, Marcus and Horse shoulder to shoulder, Marcus's mum always not more than two steps behind. They walked through the temporary main entrance, through the swing doors, under signs for various weirdly named departments and found a reception desk. The man behind the plastic screen took Marcus's card when he pushed it under the gap, then told him to head straight up, then left, second right, then … Marcus couldn't follow the rest.

'Get that?' Horse joked.

Horse led the way for all three of them. They passed the burns unit then a grey man in his dressing gown who had a drip attached to him. They saw a sign saying ENT, turned a corner and there was a waiting area. They all sat down in a row on the red plastic chairs, Marcus first, then Horse and Marcus's mum.

Marcus looked around. It was more like part of a corridor than a room. Five people were occupying five of the fifteen chairs. A sign in the area said 'No Rudeness. No Violence. Emergencies Have Priority'.

A nurse walked past, frowning, snapping off latex gloves. Hospital nursing staff wore different coloured uniforms, Marcus noticed. Some dark blue, some light blue. Other hospital staff wore no uniform as far as he could tell. They wore smart shirts or blouses, some carried stethoscopes, or clutched fluids bags, while some wielded clipboards.

For a while in the waiting area, it was like a statue contest. Nobody moved. Frustrated, Marcus got up and went up to a nurse behind a desk at the end of the corridor. 'Excuse me …'

The nurse took the card Marcus was holding out and looked at it. 'This is the STI clinic. Is that what you're here for, love?' she said, as she peered at his card, doubtfully.

'What's STI?'

He heard his mum stifle a laugh.

'Sexually Transmitted Infection,' the nurse said matter-of-factly.

'Er no,' Marcus mumbled, embarrassed.

Beside him, Horse was giggling too. Marcus nudged him and he fell silent. 'I've got a hearing test.'

'That's next left.' The nurse pointed. 'Can you see it?'

'Thanks,' said Marcus, he tugged Horse along and signalled to his mum they were on the move.

There was another long wait. The people waiting in this space were all old, except for Marcus. Eventually a nurse in dark blue walked towards him. She stopped in front of where he sat, knelt down and placed her face right in front of his.

'Are you Marcus Adenuga?'

He nodded.

'Lovely to see you, Marcus. Who's this with you?' she said, still kneeling. She had a warm Chinese face, and plucked eyebrows that danced as she spoke.

'My mate, Horse.'

'Another one wagging school? Why is hospital always so popular with school kids on a Monday morning?' she joked.

Horse squirmed.

'And this is your mum?'

Marcus nodded.

'I'm not allowed to talk,' his mum said, speaking for the first time.

The nurse winked at his mum. 'I've known that one before.'

This comment pleased his mum.

The nurse took Marcus's card. 'Just follow me will you, Marcus? Your mum and Horse can come along too, but behave or you two … get your ears syringed.' She smiled broadly as she said this. She took them to a room where another nurse was waiting. The second nurse asked Marcus to sit down then deftly looked in his ears with some kind of torch, first left ear, then right. When she released his right earlobe, she nodded to the first nurse.

'No problems there then,' the first nurse said. 'Follow me, keep up!'

They walked another twenty steps, took two turns and they came to the door of another room. The sign on it said 'Hearing 2'.

'Okay Horse and Mum, you have to wait outside now while we do the next bit. Marcus will be back out before you can say, "Ghana versus Germany."'

'Ghana versus Germany', Horse said promptly.

'Very funny,' the nurse said, wagging her finger at Horse. Even amid all his nerves, Marcus thought he liked this nurse, she was fun. She ushered him into the room. It was small and boxy, with grey walls that had nothing hanging from them, a grey ceiling and no windows. There was a small table ahead of them and one chair. The table had a set of headphones on it and what looked like a black cigarette lighter with a wire sprouting from it.

The nurse was beside him. 'Sit here,' she said gently. She picked up the cigarette lighter thing. 'This is the control,' she said. 'Pop the headphones on, Marcus, then press the red button on the top of this when you hear a sound coming through the headphones. That's all there is to it. I have to go out of the room now to set up the equipment but you'll hear my voice through the headphones very soon. Okay?'

The nurse gave him a thumbs-up once he had the headphones on then left the room.

Sat in the only chair, Marcus examined the control. It was like a wired TV remote but with only one button. He waited. There was no view but the walls, nothing to watch, no one to talk to or even to nudge.

'Can you hear me, Marcus?'

It was the nurse again, this time coming through his headphones.

'Yeh,' he said.

'Okay stand by for the sounds. You remember what to do?'

'Yeh. Press the button when I hear them.'

There was a long silence. Marcus felt his thumb slipping across the surface of the red button. Why was he not hearing anything? The grey of the room swirled and wrapped around him like a prisoner's grey blanket. Suddenly, the sounds started. They came to his left ear only.

The first one was low. Like a drone. And so loud it hurt his ear. He liked that. He could hear it so clearly. There couldn't be any problems with his ears if he could hear that sound so loud. Quickly, he clicked. The same sound came again, fainter this time, but still easy to hear. He clicked again. It came again, even fainter. Click. Then fainter still. Click. Click. Click. The sound switched to something like a submarine sonar sweep. Click. Click. Click.

He understood the pattern now: loud, then softer and softer till he could not hear them. Then back up again in volume as the nurse checked for the faintest sounds he could hear in different tones. He listened on. A referee's whistle. A boxing match bell. A Buddhist tinkly bell like his mum's relaxation CDs. The echo in a cavern when water dripped. Then … nothing. Still nothing.

At least ten seconds of nothing.

It felt like years. Why were they making him wait so long? Maybe the nurse was having a glass of water, or their equipment wasn't working.

Marcus thought maybe he heard something. He was unsure. Maybe it was the usual background sound in his ears. The low ringing he heard deep at night if he lay awake. A sound that everyone heard, didn't they? Or was it coming from the headphones?

He hesitated. Maybe he should press the button, just in case. He hesitated again. Now there was a faint, very high, ghost-like sound that he lightly felt on his eardrum, rather than heard. Or was it simply the whoosh sound of his ears and not something coming through the headphones? It was too clear to be inside his ears. He clicked. Next came a sound like the feedback from a mic but turned really low. Click.

Then a pin dropping onto a metal tray. Click. A tiny pin dropping onto a metal tray. Click. Then … nothing … nothing …

Marcus wondered if the test was over. Even as he thought this he heard that pin again. Or was it? He clicked anyway. He breathed, waited for the silence to end. The pin again. He clicked.

'Well done, Marcus, other ear now!' came the nurse's voice, loud, clear and reassuringly warm, through his headphones.

'Yeh, okay.' Marcus breathed in and readied himself. The whole series started again. It felt like an eternity. As if he was a space centre control tower, receiving signals from some remote craft on Mars. Or as if someone had suddenly invented a new Morse Code full of clicks and burrs.

Finally the nurse said he could take off the headphones. He took them off, stood and stretched his legs, but he felt faint again and had to sit down. He checked his watch. It had been only fifteen minutes.

The nurse came into the booth all smiles and waved him to follow her.

'How did I do?' Marcus asked.

'The doctor's just looking at the charts, he'll see you right now. Follow me,' she said. Marcus couldn't read anything from her tone of voice.

Horse had ducked into the room and was looking around. Marcus was so glad to see him at that moment.

'Someone likes grey,' Horse said, pointing at the walls. He picked up the headphones and popped them on,

126

then off again. He turned to Marcus. 'Bit of deejaying going on here, then?' he joked.

His mum was outside with a 'how did it go?' look on her face. Marcus shrugged an 'I dunno' back at her.

Then they were on the move, following the nurse along another glossy-floored corridor.

The nurse tapped on the door of a room called 'Consult 4', paused, swung it open and nodded to someone inside. Then she beckoned for Marcus and his mum only, to enter with her. Horse was cool about it.

'This is Marcus Adenuga. His first hearing test,' the nurse announced to the doctor.

She invited Marcus to sit down on the chair, by the doctor's desk, which he did. His mum sat on a chair further away.

The doctor was poring over a chart of wavy lines on a screen, like intersecting quadratic equations. He was a bear of a man in a too small shirt. He had a kind face behind wire glasses, and thick black hair. The doctor mumbled a thoughtful 'thank you' to the nurse.

Finally he looked up and smiled at Marcus. 'I'm Dr Glassman, you're Marcus?'

'Yeh. How did I do?' Marcus asked.

'It's not bad, and it's not all good, it's somewhere in between.'

Marcus's heart dropped. That meant …

The doctor continued: 'Your middle ear is fine. Your ear drum is perfect. The results say you are generally okay for the lower and middle range of sounds, but at the moment you won't be hearing some higher … tched sounds. Both ears … affected, the right side slight … affected than the left. You might not … picking up alarms on your mobile phone. Whistles. That kind …

thing. You hear human voices quite well, male or female, but you … struggle a little if … … or if they whisper…'

'Marcus?'

'Sorry?'

It was the doctor. He was still talking to him. Marcus tried to concentrate.

'The inner ear … where the trouble seems to be. Is there a history of deafness in your family?' the doctor said.

Marcus shook his head. His mind was as grey as the sound booth had been. Nothing stuck. Nothing made sense.

The doctor looked to his mum for confirmation of what Marcus had said. She shrugged and agreed. She had a tissue to her eyes.

'How bad will it get?' Marcus asked.

'We can't say at the moment. Is there…y deafness either on your mother's or your father's side?'

Again Marcus shook his head.

'Okay, that's not completely unusual. At the moment you need to be …ring hearing aids. They would really help out, boost the sounds you are missing out on …'

'Marcus?'

It was the nurse talking to him. Marcus did not know how long she had been calling his name. She had a hand on his shoulder. His mum was standing there as well, looking like she wanted to hug him.

'Your friend outside, Horse, should we bring him in?' the nurse asked.

Marcus nodded. He was emotionless, unsure even where he was.

'I'll bring him in then?'

Again Marcus nodded.

The next thing he knew, he and Horse were outside. His mum started hugging him and she was crying on his shoulder.

'Oh Marcus,' she wept. 'What are we going to do?'

'Mum, please.' He pulled himself away from her. 'It's okay, Mum, don't worry. But I need to think. Can I just be on my own for a moment?'

Without waiting for a reply Marcus walked away from both his mum and Horse. He started running. Horse ran after him. Marcus ran and ran until he was far away from the hospital grounds. Horse stuck with him whichever way he ran so he gave up. Next thing he knew, Horse shoved a carton of orange into his hands.

'Drink it.'

Marcus applied the drink to his lips.

'Here. A sandwich. Cheese.'

Marcus took that too and bit into it. It didn't taste of anything.

'Take this.' This time Horse shoved his ATC into his hands. 'No,' said Marcus, shoving the ball away.

'Take it,' Horse insisted.

Marcus snatched the ball from him.

He didn't know what he did the rest of that day. He remembered playing basketball with Horse in a park somewhere with his ATC. And he remembered sitting on a wall, asking, 'What am I going to do?' He didn't remember going back home but now he found himself in his bedroom by his window and his face was wet. He was staring right up at the sky. It was a black screen, with two dead screen pixels for stars. The darkness of the sky was endless. Was he about to go completely deaf? What would that be like? To not hear his own voice, or anybody else's? To not hear a dog bark, or a tree fall, or a car engine start. Or the jangle of an ice cream van?

He realised he was hungry. He didn't want to go downstairs. He remembered how, when he had sneaked in his mum had tried to follow him and he'd held his bedroom door shut. There had been a quick tussle before his mum had given up. 'This is stupid!' she'd called out, then, 'your tea's going to get cold!', before going back downstairs.

Marcus sneaked downstairs later when he thought nobody would be up. But when he got down the stairs the living room door was ajar and he heard voices. Normally he wouldn't be able to make them out, but Mum and Dad were shouting at each other and it was easy. He sat on the bottom step and listened:

'I can't take this. I've got tablets off the doctors, I'm going to have to take time off work!' said Mum.

'What about the bills?' yelled Dad. Marcus imagined him pulling his locks the way he did when he thought about money, or the lack of it.

'I'll get sick pay.'

'That won't cover the overtime you do.'

'Five Star Barry will help.'

Dad lost it big time. 'Five Star Barry? You mean one thousand-seven-hundred-and-fifty per cent Barry?'

'Who do you think pays for all the Christmas presents on this estate?' Mum raged. 'Five Star Barry!'

'If Five Star Barry's Father Christmas then Father Christmas lives on Millionaires' Row in Cheshire!'

'He provides a service.'

'The Grim Reaper provides a service!'

'Ha bloody ha!'

'Look,' Dad said, pleading now. 'They're robbing us hand over fist with that bloody card meter for the electricity. We've got two loans out for Leah's stuff. The rent is four months in arrears. Should you really be going off work?'

'My son needs me.'

'Our son needs a roof over his head.'

'I can't be dealing with this!'

Footsteps stomped. Marcus made to get up, but he was too late. His mum flung open the door.

'How long have you been sitting there?' she said, without missing a beat.

'Long enough,' replied Marcus.

Mum ploughed past him and slammed their bedroom door upstairs.

Next morning his mum sneaked into his room while he was still under the blankets. 'Are you not going to school, Marky?' she asked. She had her nicest voice on, like he was seven years old.

'No!' he groaned. He kept the quilt over his head.

'Why?'

'I don't feel well.'

'Go!'

'You can't make me.'

'I'm late already, I've got to get Leah to nursery … Just GO!'

He didn't go. He took up his PlayStation and drove cars through California for drug barons all morning. In the afternoon, he went downstairs and messed about on Facebook for a while, then searched the Internet for answers to the question: 'Deafness why does it occur?' There were a million answers, each one seeming to contradict the other. The one explanation that struck him was the one that said: 'Bad karma causes all human illnesses.' He looked up bad karma and the search engines said it was a consequence of bad acts.

He managed to avoid his mum and dad that day. He ate in his room and didn't answer when they knocked on the door. If anyone knocked for too long he called out, 'leave me alone!' and that did the trick.

That night, he lay in bed thinking about what it had said on that website. 'Bad karma causes all human illnesses'. He tried to recall all the things he'd done wrong in life. Cats he'd tried to rescue but that had fallen out of trees anyway. Windows he'd smashed with stones. Ants he'd crushed under his finger. The day he'd broken the PlayStation handset and blamed it on someone else. The neighbour's car tyres he'd let down. The art room door he'd pulled off the hinges. That fight at school when he'd punched the boy so badly blood gushed out from between his teeth … The list was endless. His deafness had to be God's way of punishing him for this. Maybe, if he promised to be on his best behaviour for the rest of his life, God would forgive him and remove his deafness? It was a glimmer of hope. A prayer formed in his mind. He was out of practice praying and had not been into church except for when his mum had once dragged him there for a christening, but he knew the basics: hands together, eyes closed. He lay in the dark in his bed and spoke softly into the dark: 'Dear God, please give me my hearing back and I will never do anything wrong ever again. Amen.'

He opened his eyes. He waited for a flash of lightning or a roll of thunder, a sign that God had heard. There was nothing. But he was still hopeful. After all, He must get a lot of these requests. He couldn't be letting off thunder and lightning every time a request headed His way, otherwise there'd be a permanent storm in the sky. A text came through from Adele.

Bored. Wot u doin?
Nuttin. Goin 2 slep
Nity nite (This came with a picture of a sleeping panda)

Adele's sleeping panda eased him into sleep.

Next day Marcus woke eagerly. Had his deal with God come good yet? He tried his phone's alarm. He still couldn't hear it. He turned the kettle on and sat in the living room. His dad could hear the kettle click off from there. He waited. After four minutes of not hearing a click, he went into the kitchen. It had clicked off and he hadn't heard. In desperation, he found some old newspaper, set it alight using the cooker's gas ring, then let it burn under the kitchen smoke alarm. He heard the smoke alarm go off clearly. But he had always heard the smoke alarm go off, what he didn't hear was the little blip sound it made when its battery needed replacing. His mum and dad heard that, even Leah did, he'd noticed, but not him.

The newspaper was still burning on the kitchen floor where he'd dropped it. It was a swirling fire now. He jumped on the flames and stamped them out. There were scorch marks on his trousers. They would wash out. He scooped up the burnt newspaper and threw it into the back yard then ran a cloth under a tap and mopped the burn marks off the kitchen tiles. He didn't usually hear the tap running at the sink, he realised. But that deal with God, maybe, maybe it had come good. Had he left it on? Could he hear it? No, there was nothing.

Maybe the tap was off. He turned to look. The tap was on. Despondent, Marcus rinsed out the cloth, chucked it in the wash basin, wrenched the tap shut till the water stopped then ran upstairs. He put his hands together and cursed God: 'God, I'll leave you if you don't fix my ears. Fix them else you're a fraud!'

He waited to be struck down by lightning. Or to suddenly hear things he had not been able to hear. Neither happened. He beat his bed with his fists in rage.

Next day his mum burst into the room in the morning and ranted at him, saying he had to get up, even tugged at his quilt. But he held on tight and she gave up. He felt the house shake as the front door slammed. He waited to make sure she did not suddenly double back, then got dressed, and left the house. He did not know where he was going. He had forgotten his coat. He didn't go back for it. He felt feverish anyway.

He found a back street cafe full of builders in yellow bibs and ordered an all-day breakfast. He had never wagged school before. It felt good. He had joined the elite club of kids who didn't do school. He practised his rebel scowl.

'That sausage a bit chewy, love?' said the cafe lady.

'Nah, it's fine.'

He got out his phone and on a whim, texted Adele.

What u doin?

Lunch brek. Bored. Send me a pic

Marcus sent a selfie. Adele texted him back straight away.

That not skul. Why u deh?

Sad. Had enuf

Turn on location on yr fone.

134

Marcus did. Then texted her the name of the café: Jills Eats.

Stay deh. Am close.

Marcus chewed on his sausage and chased some of the hard baked beans on his plate. Would Adele really come? The big cafe window had a picture of a bearded man eating a hamburger painted onto it. The paint was beginning to peel so only half the hamburger was left. There was a hot air blower above the entrance door that triggered whenever someone came in, which was only every five minutes. Marcus pulled at a piece of sausage stuck between his teeth.

Four hot air blows later, Adele arrived. He saw her jump out of a taxi. She was still in her uniform. He stood up so she would see him, and suddenly felt embarrassed. Was this a date? It couldn't be a date, they were in a greasy spoon cafe. What was it then?

'So,' she said, sitting at his table. 'What's sad?'

He shook his head. 'Don't know where to start. I'm in hell.'

'Even hell's got to have better wallpaper than this.' She was looking around. The wallpaper was hung badly and the clashing purple stripes with pink dots didn't do anything to brighten the interior.

'You're not helping,' Marcus said.

'Sorry. Focus.' She placed her hands to either side of her face to create a finger tunnel and looked at him through that tunnel. 'What's up?'

He felt his eyes welling so he looked up to balance the water on his eyeballs and make sure it didn't become tears. There was a fan attached to the cafe light fitting. The fan's propellers looked like they hadn't moved in years and were coated with grease, with fluff stuck on top. He was tempted to pull the cord that dangled down to switch the thing on. If he stood on his chair he could reach it.

Adele kicked him under the table. 'Look at me, Marcus. What's up?'

He sighed. Weird how her kicking him made him feel better. Like taking a cold shower. He told her about his ordeal at the hospital, the hearing test booth, the result. Her hands were down now and she was really listening.

'You must have felt awful,' she said.

He nodded, biting his lip.

The cafe lady turned up with her ordering pad and looked at Adele. She had impatient fingers. 'Ready?'

'I'll have a non-fat chocolate brownie frappucinno with ice,' said Adele.

'How about a hot chocolate with squirty cream on top?' The lady gave Adele a look that said, 'I'd love to throw you out.'

'Hot chocolate with squirty cream on top would be amazing,' Adele said. 'Thanks so much.'

'Three pounds.'

Adele placed three pound coins on the table.

'Hot chocolate, squirty cream, Saqib!' she shouted, taking the coins, then she moved on to the next table.

Marcus hadn't yet paid himself. He wondered why the cafe lady had made Adele pay up front.

Adele prompted him out of his thoughts. 'And your mum and dad are no help?'

Marcus grimaced. 'I mean, they try but they're too all over me. They don't understand.'

'The way you described it, reminds me of when the neighbour's little cat got itself stuck in our w ... shing machine.'

'Wishing machine?'

Adele smiled at his mistake. 'Noo, washing machine.'

'Oh.' He was glad she hadn't laughed when he'd misheard, even though he himself found the mishearing funny: Wishing machine. That was exactly what he needed right now, a giant wishing machine.

Adele was still on her cat story; he only half-listened to her. He didn't really mind what she said, it was her being with him that made him feel better somehow. Why was that? He looked across at Adele and tried to concentrate.

'... then we found her there after three days: Barely alive. Her eyes all gone, you know, like ...' She searched for the word.

'That's how you look, Marcus. Like the cat in the washing machine.' She rolled her eyes around.

'Umm.' Marcus spent a moment trying to picture the cat.

'Umm?' she said.

'Disorientated, you mean? The cat?'

'That's it. I knew you'd know the word. Disorientated. You look disorientated.'

He laughed, pleased with himself for knowing the word she had been searching for. Adele placed her hand over his on the table and squeezed it. 'Listen, I have to get back for stupid afternoon registration. But I'm here for you. Always.' She leaned across the table and kissed him on the cheek. Before he had time to react, she got up. 'And you smell nice today,' she said. 'For once!'

He watched her leave. A taxi from the same firm that dropped her off nosed up to the kerb outside. It had to have been waiting there. She got in and was gone.

Marcus left three pounds fifty on the table for what he ate. 'Keep the change!' he called out, feeling big. He remembered the scowl he had entered the cafe with, stuck it back on his face and kept it going as he walked into the wind again. Yes, he was a rebel, he thought. He'd skipped school all week. He actually had a girlfriend. Sort of. He only needed to start hot-wiring cars to complete his transition to ASBO kid. Yet he missed school. All his mates were there. He walked aimlessly along street after street till it was dark.

His mum and dad were waiting for him when he got back.

'Marcus, we have to talk,' said Mum, immediately all over him.

Marcus groaned.

'We phoned the GP,' said Dad, all wise and know-it-all. 'He's got the results from the hospital. They've diagnosed you have a hearing problem.'

'No! Really?' said Marcus.

'It must be hard but we'll support you, son,' his dad intoned, ignoring or not noticing his sarcasm.

'Shut up, Dad. What do you care!' Marcus blurted. 'All you're bothered about is your singing!'

'That's not true, Marcus,' Dad said.

'Marky, you've got me worried. You're my baby, I can't bear to see you so unhappy,' Mum intervened.

'I'm not your baby, Leah's your baby! Now leave. Me. Alone!'

Marcus shot up into his bedroom and locked his door before his mum had a chance to add anything.

He didn't remember sleeping but the Thursday morning daylight woke him and he realised he had felt the front door slam twice, which meant both Mum and Dad had left. After getting so cold the other day, he wasn't so keen on walking the streets anymore; his fever was worse. He decided to see how long he could stay in bed. He made it to late afternoon. At 3:27 pm he sneaked down before anyone got back and raided the fridge, then bolted himself back in his bedroom. He managed to stay that whole evening in his room.

On Friday morning, after his parents had left, Marcus got up. His mum had pushed a note under his door:

Dear Marcus,
Please talk to me. I can't bear it when you won't talk, it makes me upset. I am not sure my heart can take it any more. I'm sorry if I did anything wrong. Please tell me how I can help you.
Much love
Mum
XXX

It was a typical Mum note, full of emotional blackmail. When he went downstairs, there was another note, this time from his dad, on the coffee table:

Hi Marcus, U like the yeti at mo. Can u fix my computer so I can record myself singing tracks direct using the webcam? Thanks. Think about getting back to school, yeah? Lunch in freezer. Third shelf from top. Your favourite. Ham and pineapple.

For some reason, he switched the computer on and fixed the recording software for his dad. It took all of fifteen seconds. His dad was an idiot.

Marcus really did not want to talk to either of them. What could they do to help? It was *his* ears involved not theirs. Still, he didn't like the idea of his mum getting upset. So he left his own note on the table:

Mum, I will talk to you tomorrow morning.

MARCUS, BEETHOVEN AND FAT BOY SLIM

Saturday morning. It was time to face the music. Marcus got dressed slowly and tiptoed down. To his surprise, his dad was there at the table as well as his mum, and they weren't arguing. His mum had her anxious face on. Dad just looked bored.

'Well?' Marcus said, helping himself to the porridge with jam his mum must have made for him.

'I can understand you being down in the dumps, Marky.'

'You can't let this little setback stop you,' Dad chipped in.

Marcus sighed. 'You don't get it do you? I'm deaf. I might as well be dead!'

'You're hearing me aren't you?' said Dad.

Marcus decided the best thing to do was ignore his dad. His dad was not worth the effort. He turned to his mum. 'You were there. They say I have to wear hearing aids.'

'Beethoven was deaf,' Dad weighed in again. 'And that DJ Fat Boy Slim's got hearing problems. And this old time singer called Johnnie Ray wore a hearing aid, his nickname —'

141

'Dad you're not helping.'

Mum shushed Dad. 'No, you're not.'

'Don't shush me,' Dad said to Mum.

Marcus made to get up. The two of them were starting again. He didn't see why he had to listen to it.

'Marcus, wait!' his mum said, looking like she was about to cry. He sat down again.

'Marcus, I want to help you,' Mum said. 'Tell me what I can do to help. You can't spend every day in your bedroom on your PlayStation.'

'Why not?'

'Because it's not healthy. We have to deal with this,' Mum said. 'The doctor's signed me off work for blood pressure. I can't take it, Marcus, I can't bear to see you so unhappy.'

Then his mum's tears started. Marcus sighed. He knew it would happen. And he had no defence against it. Dad put his arm around Mum then went to make her a cup of tea. 'Don't cry, Mum,' Marcus said. He placed his hand on her shoulder for a second. Then he went to his bedroom.

THE FITTING

In the morning he came down and went into the kitchen. The back door was open. He saw his mum bent over something and heard this banging. His mum loved DIY. Glad he had heard the sound, he went outside to see what she was up to.

'Just in time,' she said when she saw him.

'Are you alright, Mum?'

'Ta da!' She stepped back and did that show business razzle thing with her hands.

Marcus looked. 'What is it?'

It was a two metre square piece of board with square holes cut in it.

'Guess!' she said.

Marcus shook his head. He had no idea. 'Giant cat flap?' he guessed.

'Wait. I forgot.' His mum dashed inside the kitchen and came out with three wooden circles with target rings painted on them in black and white, like archery targets. She attached the circles to metal hooks sticking out of each of the cat flaps. 'There. Now guess!' she said with another razzle.

He was going to say: 'Cat flap for very blind cats that needed targets to find the door', but he didn't want to see his mum looking disappointed. He hesitated. He still hadn't got a clue.

'Football?' she hinted.

'Okay!' He'd got it now. 'Target practice? You shoot it in the holes?' He remembered mentioning it to her how when he'd been to the football academy training ground he'd seen one and it was brilliant. 'Thanks, Mum.'

His mum wasn't finished. 'Not any old target practice. Try it, see what happens.'

She rolled a ball to Marcus.

Marcus stepped away a bit, flipped the ball up, let it bounce on his knee then hit the ball at the lowest target. It shot into the first square, hitting it dead on. A panel popped up out of the top of the board with a hand and the word 'Yes!'painted on it. It made Marcus laugh.

'I knew you'd like it.' his mum said and rolled the ball to him again. 'Next one.'

The middle target had a smaller square hole so it was tougher. He took aim, hit it and a hand shot up again, this time with 'Yes! Yes!' on it.

The third one was a smaller square again, and higher up. He took a short run up and smacked that one right on the money. 'Yes! Yes! Yes!' shot up.

'You like?' his mum asked.

'It's ace, Mum,' he said.

'Do I get a hug, then?'

He gave his mum the longest, tightest hug he'd ever given her. She laughed in his arms. 'Let go, I can't breathe!' she cried.

As his mum glowed with pride, Marcus looked around the board. 'What are those?' he asked, pointing out some small panels attached to the back of the board.

'Oh, I rigged these birthday card chips that make a cheering noise. I forgot you wouldn't hear them. I'll work out a way to get them boosted.'

'No, that's great, Mum. You know, thoughtful. I love you, Mum.'

'Now don't get me going again.'

'Are you going through the menopause, Mum?'

His mum startled. 'Why do you say that?'

'We did it in school. They say women cry a lot for no reason at that time. And get hot.'

'No, my eggs are fine and popping out regularly, thanks for your concern.'

'That's okay.'

'It's good then?'

Marcus grinned. 'I'm loving it. What did you make it out of?'

'Wood, wire, hinges. You know. Stuff.'

'You're a genius, Mum. You're the best Mum ever.'

She smiled at him. 'Don't be outside too long, it's cold.'

He spent the rest of the day milking the target board's applause, left foot then right. He didn't mind the holes were square instead of round.

Marcus's mum had arranged for him to go to the hearing clinic the next Monday to get moulds taken of his ears so they could make the hearing aids. Meanwhile, since he was off school, she took time off work. Although he moaned about it, it was okay knocking about the house with his mum. She stuck to him like Luigi to Mario in *Super Mario Land*. They had watched the *Jeremy Kyle Show* together and some other rubbish. She told him about her plans for her magician's act and tried out card tricks on him. She was pretty useless at them, but that was why she needed to practice.

The time for the clinic came. His mum went with him. It was a squat building crammed between some wasteland and a supermarket car park. There was a tiny reception space with the usual plastic chairs arranged in a row. Behind the glass screen was a woman in a white, nursey type of uniform who spoke to Marcus's mum. Before he had time to park himself in a chair, Marcus was whisked through with his mum to a room marked 'Fitting 3'.

A stranger's warm hands began tugging at his ears, first the left one then the right then he felt some cold, pink goo being poured into each ear in turn. He felt it harden quickly. The man pressed it out and tapped him on the shoulder 'All done,' he said.

Two days later, Marcus was back at the clinic with his mum to get the hearing aids fitted. This time there was a different man. He wore a tie, and had a suitcase of equipment. He asked Marcus a few questions to confirm his identity and make sure he had no colds. Then he pulled out a box that looked vaguely as though it should have a wedding ring inside. When the man opened the box, two hearing aids sat inside the box, on a purple silk pad.

'These are the "all in the ear" type, Marcus, so they are very small,' the technician said. 'They work very well and people can hardly see them. Shall I pop them in your ears and you can have a listen?'

Marcus looked to his mum. His Mum had that look on her face with the chin lowered that meant he did not have a choice.

The technician placed them inside Marcus's ears.

Marcus shook his head. 'No difference,' he said.

The technician smiled. 'That's because I haven't switched them on yet.' He leaned over Marcus again and pressed some button on each of the things in his ears.

'Marcus can you hear something?'

Marcus smiled. 'Mum, do you always talk that loud?'

'Can you hear this?' Mum asked again from behind his back.

'It's your keys.' She was jangling them.

His mum nodded. Marcus looked again. She was leaking tears.

'Mum, don't.' Marcus wanted to vanish.

'He's a remarkable lad, to have coped so well for so long. He's probably been lip-reading without knowing it,' the technician said to Marcus's mum. Then, 'Marcus, I've set them low for now, while you get used to the new sound.'

'You mean they get louder?'

'Yes, we can turn them up a little more when you come back, and slowly get them to full volume.'

Mum was dabbing her eyes. 'He's cured,' she sobbed.

'Things will be better for him, Mrs Adenuga, but it's not a cure. Marcus, your brain has to get used to the new information, the new sounds. So try to keep them in as much as possible. Remove them for gym, sports and other physical activities.'

'Like football?'

'All sports, really. And obviously they are electronic devices so you can't take showers or baths with them in. You shouldn't sleep in them either, or feed them to the dog.'

'What was that last one?' Mum said, as she patted her eyes with a tissue.

The technician smiled. 'You wouldn't believe how many young people come back and say "sorry the dog ate them". It seems dogs have an appetite for these things.'

A desk phone jangled. The technician picked it up. He said three 'ahs', two 'okays' and a small sigh before putting the phone down again. 'Have a go at putting them in and out yourself now, Marcus.'

Marcus placed them in his ears. It was quite easy. They felt cold in his ears and his ears felt blocked, the way your nose felt when you had a cold.

'Good,' said the technician. 'Feel for the on-off switch for both of them.' The technician guided Marcus's fingers. 'That's on. And again. Excellent that's off. Switch them on again. Okay, that's it. We're done here. Do you want to leave them in now?'

That look from his mum again.

'Here's a guide book to help you. You'll still miss the occasional word, but you'll hear much better. We'll book you another appointment for six weeks' time and see how you've been getting on.'

The technician was already shaking his mum's hand before Marcus had a chance to open the guide book. Marcus saw why as they crossed the reception area again to leave. There were about twelve people waiting on and around the chairs.

Marcus wore the hearing aids, switched off, on the bus ride home. It felt like he had a hippo in each ear. He looked to see if other people were staring. He sank his neck down and pulled in his shoulders, then realised that he was wearing a hoodie, so he flicked the hood up. All the while, his mum was chatting to him about this and that. He nodded along, not listening.

Back home, Dad popped off his headphones and greeted him, beaming like an idiot.

'How did it go?'

Marcus ignored him and took the stairs to the privacy of his own room. He waited to see if he had been followed. When he was certain he had not, he switched his hearing aids on and listened.

A car starting.

Voices of some children playing outside.

A distant ambulance siren.

A sudden chorus of dogs like a full canine conversation.

The radiator in his room rattling. He placed his hand on the radiator and it stopped rattling. He took his hand off. It rattled. On. Off. He amused himself making a radiator tune up from the rattle. He'd never heard it rattle before. He sang to the rhythm of the radiator tune. 'Rattle rat rattle rat rattle.'

His own voice sounded eerie. He tried some words out. His own name. 'Marcus'. It sounded like someone was shouting his name with a distorted megaphone. He tried out the vowel sound in the first syllable of his name: 'Mar Mar. Mar.' It sounded more squeaky than usual. He didn't like it. He hadn't expected this. He tried saying a few other words aloud. Every word he said sounded squeaky or boomy or sometimes both squeaky and boomy. He felt the blood beating in his head as his frustration rose. Then the technician's voice came to him: 'It will take you some time to adjust'. Clinging to that thought, he went downstairs, less keen to talk to anyone than ever before.

All the doors in the house squeaked. Why hadn't somebody oiled them?

He whizzed through to the kitchen, unlocked the back door and went outside, taking his ATC with him.

He tried some volleys. When he hit the ball hard it made a firm smack sound he hadn't heard before. He heard the corner house dog scrabbling as he practised. And somewhere above, there were birds singing. It was the first time in ages he had heard birds. Amazing. He looked and looked for them but could not see them.

He came back inside the house wondering whether he was going to be asked a ton of questions, but his mum just patted the sofa next to her. She was watching a soap. Marcus sat next to her for a bit then wandered off and listened to new sounds around the house. That water running out of the kitchen tap. The slithery sound of clingfilm when you tore it off the roll. He fried an egg and listened to the fat spit and explode. He had never known how the kettle rumbled for ages before actually clicking off. The funniest was the gurgling of Leah's tummy. He fed her, listening to the funny smack sound of her lips as she sucked on the plastic spoon laden with gooey porridge, then this *gurgle gurgle gurgle*. The bathroom was a chamber of strange and unusual sounds, some of them made by himself, some of them caused by all the piping. He sighed as he got into bed. It had been one momentous day.

Next morning Marcus got up early for football practice. He pulled on his tracksuit, his trainers, fished his ATC from under his pillow and took off for the pitch. There was a drizzly rain, more a fog than rain, but it didn't trouble him. He spotted his dad on the other side of the pitch, coming back from a shift at the post office sorting depot. Marcus waved. 'On my head, son!' his dad signalled, running towards him.

Marcus booted the ball high towards his dad. His dad came running for it, leaping up at the last moment. The ball skidded off his dad's head and bounced onto a discarded piece of garden fence. His dad retrieved the ball with his hands and tried juggling it with his feet all the way to Marcus. Marcus watched, amused. The most he could say of his dad's ball skills was that he was enthusiastic. When Marcus got the ball back he did a quick run through his repertoire of tricks. It was the first time in ages his dad had watched him. His dad's eyes stretched.

'That's out of this world. Your footballing skills. You had to have … it from me.' He didn't catch the word after 'have'. Without his hearing aids he realised how many gaps there were in simple conversation.

'But you're rubbish, Dad.'

'My skills lay dormant, son. In you they have awoken.'

'Whatever,' Marcus laughed. He kicked the ball back to his dad and his dad tried a few step overs before booting it back. They played for twenty minutes, his dad in goal, Marcus trying shots from various angles before they went back home together. It was Saturday, Mum had taken Leah to a car boot sale at a local church. His dad made them both breakfast.

'Why don't you ever show up at my matches, Dad?' Marcus asked over fried egg sandwiches.

'I'm in training for *Britain's …t Talent*,' said Dad. 'Wait till I win. Then you'll be proud of me.'

'But Dad, you're my dad. I'm proud of you anyway. You're the best dad I've got.'

'The only dad you've got.'

'Right!' Marcus smiled. They both laughed.

'So,' said Dad, 'how's the ears thing going?'

'It's okay.'

'Wear them today though, there's a … lad, the doctors have said you have to get used to them, right?'

'I don't want to.'

'Do it anyway.'

'No!'

'Marcus! Are you not wearing them? Get them in. Now!'

'Jeez.' Marcus stomped off to his bedroom, prised open the case and rammed the hearing aids in his ears. It vexed him to wear them. Everything jangled when he put them in. He came back downstairs in a foul mood. 'Satisfied?'

His dad hadn't even noticed. He was flicking though DVD's in his music library. Marcus slumped into the computer chair. He and his dad had been getting on fine. Why did his dad have to go and spoil it?

Suddenly Marcus's head fried with pain. A noise electrocuted his brain. From the speakers. He screamed out, 'Stop! Dad! Dad!'

But his dad had his headphones on and couldn't hear him. Marcus went up to his dad and shook his shoulder. His dad shrugged him off. 'Two minutes,' he mimed, pointing to the playtime on the audio editor screen.

'I can't take it! I can't take it! You're killing me!' Tears streamed down Marcus's face. He burst out of the living room and wrestled with the front door till he managed to fling it open. He turned and saw his dad getting off his chair and calling out to him, but he kept on running.

RUNNING

Marcus ran out into the street. His head throbbed. The words of the technician repeated in his brain: 'It will take you some time to adjust. It will take you some time to adjust.' He cursed the technician.

Where was he going? He didn't know, he just ran. Cars blared and churned through the rain. A traffic light crossing bleeped. An air conditioning fan roared by the chip shop. Somewhere someone was going at a sheet of metal with a hammer. It was a mad cacophony. At least while he kept his hearing aids in; which he had to. The technician said. His mum said. His dad said. Everyone said. He felt he was no longer human. They had made him into an android, part human, part machine. Everything slammed or squeaked or hissed. Yet when he took the hearing aids out everything was frighteningly quiet. He found a park, sat down on a bench. He was panting. His breathing sounded to himself like a bear in a cave. He wanted to see Adele. He texted her. She said she was alone and gave him the house number and post code. He switched his phone's GPS on and keyed in the post code. He knew which bus to catch, he'd seen her get on it enough times. He got off at the last stop then let his phone's GPS system guide him.

He walked along a curving, unlit road. It had huge houses to either side, each one set back behind trees or gates or tall railings. There were no street lights, but as he walked he triggered security lights everywhere along the road. They blinded him. He breathed in deep, determined not to give up.

Finally he was at a tall white wooden gate which had the number thirty-eight on it. A huge white house loomed behind the gates. There was a bell in the brick pillar. Marcus pressed it. He didn't hear it ring but Adele's voice came from somewhere inside the pillar.

'Hiya – come in!'

From somewhere, a ghostly, synthetic voice whined 'enter'. The gates whirred open. Small lights set in the ground lit up a gravel path to the house door. Marcus crunched up the path. Adele was waiting for him by the door.

'I can't believe you've come here.'

'Is it okay?'

'It's just me. C'mon.'

Adele hurried him inside and closed the door. In the hallway, everything was three times as big as it was in his own house and blinged to the max. Gold wallpaper. Chandelier. Lush cream carpet. And that was just the hallway. She led him through rooms into the kitchen. It was funny, he thought. For all the bling, her kettle was the same as theirs.

'What have you been up to then?' Adele quizzed. 'You look upset.'

'This and that,' Marcus replied. He wondered how Adele could read him so well. He put his hands behind his head, kicked back on his chair and tried to look more chilled. 'You've got a nice place here.'

'I wish I could be more like you.'

'What, like banned from doing the thing you love doing most?'

'You've been really cool about it. You haven't done anything stupid like burned down the school.'

'I'm considering it.'

There was a silence. Adele looked at him a long time.

'Are you going to tell me then?' she asked finally.

'What?'

'What's troubling you?'

Marcus sighed. 'You not noticed anything?'

'What?'

'Look at my ears. Carefully.'

Adele looked. She finally noticed. 'What are those?'

'Hearing aids. I have to wear hearing aids.'

'And?'

'I don't know. I'm scared I'll get teased. Evan will get hold of it and it will be endless.'

'Who's Evan?'

'The class clown. Him and Jamil.'

'Don't let a couple of fools spoil your life.'

'You don't get it. I don't want to wear them.'

'You're wearing them now, aren't you? And I couldn't tell.'

She kissed him roughly on the cheek as she took up his empty pasta plate. He hadn't noticed she'd set any food in front of him, and didn't remember eating it.

'What was that for?'

'You've come here, even though you know what my dad's like.'

Truth was, he'd forgotten about her dad. 'You really don't notice them?' Marcus asked, fingering his earlobes.

'No. Now let's talk about me!'

That was Adele all over. 'How many rooms have you got in this house?' he asked.

'About sixteen. It's all borrowed money. And we'll have to move soon. The-Bank-Of-Dad is about to go belly up. Let's go watch TV.'

Adele led him into the lounge. It was like something out of the Titanic. It took two chandeliers to light it. There was a silver and glass coffee table as long as a small boat. A huge, silver mantelpiece, with a built in clock and fancy mirror stared back at him. There was a mega TV up on a wall. They sat together on the white leather sofa in the middle of the lounge watching rubbish. Marcus played with the hearing aid settings, making the TV sound go louder then quieter until he was comfortable with it.

'What are you doing?' she asked.

'I've got my own volume control.'

She laughed and shuffled closer to him. Marcus listened to his breathing steady itself. He felt Adele's shoulder slide into his, and he brought his arm around her. She began arguing with the TV and threw a cushion at it, so he tickled her ribs to make her calm down. She fought him for a bit then gave up and settled into him even more. He loved the scent of her and her warmth in his arms. Marcus tried and tried but he couldn't keep his eyelids open. He switched his hearing aids off.

Suddenly there was shouting. '… heck going on? … come home… past midnight … half undressed … sight … sick.' Marcus's brain scrambled. Where was he? He roused himself through a fog of sleep.

'Adele! What the hell … you doing!'

'Dad, he's my boyfriend, get over it! And don't come running your mouth to me … what time it is. Most times you stay out all night!'

Marcus knew where he was now. At Adele's. Adele had been wrapped up in his arms, her head on his chest. She was still there, pretty much. Her dad was towering above them. The clock in the mantelpiece said ten minutes past midnight. He switched his hearing aids back on.

'Boyfriend? Is that true, Marcus?' Mr Vialli asked him directly. His neck veins were popping. A big vein in the middle of his face looked like it was about to burst.

'Yes,' Marcus said defiantly to Mr Vialli. He shifted himself upright on the sofa.

'Over my dead body is my daughter dating a black boy. Get out of here, go on, scram!'

'Fuck you, you racist wanker!' said Marcus, standing up and making Mr Vialli leap back.

'Yeah Dad, throw a bit of casual racism into the mix, why not? You are so pig ignorant!' Adele shouted, getting up herself.

'I'm your dad, and I make the decisions round here!' her dad shouted back.

'Speak to the hand.'

Marcus had had enough. 'Leave it, Adele,' he said.

He brushed past Mr Vialli and Mr Vialli jumped back again as though Marcus had thrown a punch at him. Marcus wanted to deck him even though Mr Vialli was twice his size. Instead he fled the room. He went down a corridor. He passed a grandfather clock that went 'dong!' making him jump. This wasn't the way. He corrected himself and went the other way. He found the front door, flung it open and turned, expecting Adele to be behind him. But there was only her father at a doorway, mouthing off at him. Marcus gave him the V sign, slammed the house door shut then ran up the driveway to the gate. The gravel crunched like bones grinding together. He couldn't see a handle so he leapt for the top of the gate and dragged himself up then flung himself over. He heard something rip when he landed, but he didn't feel any pain. He scrambled up and hurried along the road. Security lights fired at him from all sides as he ran.

His mind was on fire. Where was he running to? His ears were ringing like he was trapped in a church bell tower and someone below was pulling all the bell ropes, making him fall against the bells. *Clang! Clang! Clang!* Cars roared by like planes taking off.

He saw a silent mass of dark water in a gap between houses. Adele had said she lived by a river. Marcus ran towards it. He slid down the river bank. Reeds broke like ball bearings cannoning into each other underfoot, raising a stink of swamp. Brambles snagged at him, their coils snapping like mouse traps as he broke through them.

He halted at the river's edge and looked down at the water. Even a river rat had a better life than him. He grabbed reeds, rocks and clumps of earth and threw them into the water. He heard the water make a gulping sound, swallowing them, leaving no trace.

He tilted back his head to the sky and cursed God. 'Fuck you, God!' He screamed at the river. He slumped down with his head in his hands by the water's edge. The pain he felt inside himself was unbearable. His school had betrayed him over the football. The only thing that had kept him going was football. And they had taken it away. Miss Podborsky had made sure of it. Then Leonard had made doubly sure. It was so unfair. And what did his parents do about it? Sweet F. A. His parents might as well be aliens for all the use they were to him. They never fought for him, just sailed along with their stupid lives. And what was Adele's game back at her house? He'd expected her to follow him out but she'd deserted him for her racist dad right at the moment when he needed her most. Did she even like him as a person? Or was he simply a way to tease her brother and annoy her dad? To top it all, his ears were well and truly fucked. Why keep going?

He looked at the river then up along the bank, tracing the trail of reeds he'd crushed sliding down. Did he want to go up there again, to deal with all that stuff, when he could dive into the water here, sink like the clumps of earth and be gone? He preferred down here. He could finish it. He hoped Podborsksy and Ozone felt bad if he did. There. See what you did. He hoped the guilt sat on them like a toad for the rest of their lives. Maybe it would do some good, stop them ruining some other kid's life.

In some bizarre way, he enjoyed the thought. In his mind, he wrote a letter to his parents.:

Dear Mum and Dad,
I'm sorry. I can't take anymore. Give Leah my old Teddy under my bed. Darryl McCaulay (Horse) can have my ATC if he wants it. Don't blame yourselves. It's easier for everyone this way. Please don't be sad. Marcus. XXXX

That was his message. He took out his phone and typed it in.

The river didn't scare him. He heard it whispering by as its heavy waters shifted along. It was ironic, that he heard those waters now. His hearing aids had given him that, maybe they might give him other things. He looked at the river again. Did he really want to jump in? It would be cold and muddy.

Whooooooooooosh.

A shadow threw itself at him. It knocked him back into the reeds, bundled its way up, over and around him then almost knocked him into the river. It span round and bit into his trousers, tugging. A brute of a shadow.

'Nero!'

Nero growled, still tugging at Marcus in the direction of the upper river bank.

'What are you doing?' Marcus exclaimed. He clambered up the bank, Nero still clamped to his trousers, snarling.

When he was fully up on the bank, Nero let go of him, but nudged him, then bounded up to the top. Nero looked down at Marcus, wagging his tail as if to say, 'Come on, faster, you humans are so slow!'

Marcus scrambled up through the reeds and brambles. He grabbed Nero's head, kissed him and wiped the slobber from Nero's mouth. Nero was panting badly. He pressed into Marcus again, wanting him to keep moving.

'Alright, Nero, calm it down.'

They left the river. The dog trotted on, turning every few steps to make sure Marcus was following. It wasn't long before the streets became familiar.

As he turned the corner into his street, he saw a police car parked outside their house. His mum was leaning on the garden wall under the streetlight. She saw him and came charging up. Marcus smiled as he heard his mum's voice, even though she was raging. 'What kind of disappearing act was that? Where have you been? Look at the state of you! I've been worried sick. You are in deep trouble.'

His mum pulled up abruptly. There was a sound like a scene from *Day of The Triffids*.

Marcus looked down. Nero was baring his teeth and growling. He hadn't liked Marcus's mum's manner.

'Easy, Nero, it's only my mum,' Marcus said.

The snarling stopped but Nero's ears stayed up, and his body still leaned forwards, alert, ready to spring.

Marcus's dad appeared out of the police car with a mobile phone stuck to his ear, shouting: 'It's fine, we've found him, tell everyone to stop looking!' A woman he did not know came out of Marcus's house carrying a wailing Leah and handed her to Marcus's dad who stuck his thumb in Leah's mouth to stop her crying. Meanwhile, word was spreading that he had been found and even though it was the middle of the night, cars began pulling up left, right and centre. Marcus watched, amazed at all the commotion. People were hugging him, perfect strangers were patting him on the back. Nero's owner opened his door, looked across and whistled for his dog. The sound came sharp to Marcus's ears this time. He wondered how much sharper Nero heard it. Nero lifted his head but didn't move. Instead the dog looked at Marcus. 'It's okay, go on boy,' said Marcus.

Nero left Marcus's side and, tail lowered, sloped over to Mr Winstanley's house. Marcus felt sorry for the dog. He watched Nero till he was lost in the shadows of Mr Winstanley's front garden.

'Thanks, Mr Winstanley!' Marcus's mum called out.

'Glad he's good for something!' Nero's owner shouted back.

Then his mum was all over Marcus. Telling him off and hugging him at the same time.

Marcus glanced at his watch. It was 1.34 am. The whole street was awake. He felt foolish and embarrassed. Out of the crowd, Horse appeared. 'Hey bro, where've you been?' Horse clasped his shoulder. Leonard popped up alongside him, then Ira and Jamil. 'We had a search party going,' said Horse. 'Was fun, man, best time in ages. Where were you?'

Marcus's mum pulled Marcus away from them. 'Marcus, can we take this inside?' She turned to everyone still outside and said: 'You've all been great, but it's all over now. Go and get some sleep, yeah? It's a family matter now. Go home. Go to your beds!'

His mum's voice had a strained edge to it, a tone he'd never heard before. Marcus knew he was in deep trouble. He walked into the house and took off straight to his bedroom. He listened to the many voices downstairs. He also heard, Karen, the neighbour's teenaged daughter, singing in her bedroom behind his own bedroom wall. The cars must have woken her up and she'd decided to join in the fun. She sang the same song again and again till her mum yelled. She told her mum to fuck off but went quiet. Sometimes Karen's house was as crazy as his. Marcus shifted on his bed. The bed's bolts needed tightening, it had a thousand squeaky joints. His own breathing was so loud he wondered if he was becoming asthmatic. Then he remembered, it was the hearing aids that were creating this whole new world of sound. He started playing with his breathing, trying out the different sounds he could make by breathing in different ways – through his mouth, through his noise, inhaling for a long time, exhaling in short bursts.

It was like turned down beat boxing. He was getting his breathing ready for when the shouting would start, probably in the morning once his mum had recovered. He felt his phone vibrate. Adele.

Where r u? U ok?

Fine

Cum 2 yr window, luk outside

Marcus got off his bed and peeped out. He saw someone waving. It was Adele, partly hidden by the neighbour's car. He was astonished. He could see her texting him madly.

This is so romeo n juliet

Yeh

Ecpt yr on balcony not the girl – me

Lol

I luv u 2 bits. Just so u no.

Marcus smiled and did a heart shape for her from his window. He texted her:

Go now, b4 u get in trouble. Mum and Dad mad here. Yr Dad gona go nuts 2

OK. I woz worried. Wantd to no u ok. Soz abt my dad agen

How u get bak?

Will get taxi. I pay him w dads credit card lol

She waved a square at him that he guessed was her dad's credit card. She texted him again.

C ya x

Marcus blew her a kiss from the window then watched her walk into the shadows.

Adele. She was a whole new symphony on his life.

It was well past midnight but Marcus could still hear lots of noises coming from downstairs. He clenched his fists for courage then went downstairs. Dad was there with a policeman. The policeman asked: 'Are you okay, Marcus?'

'Yeh.'

'Okay, I'll leave you lot to it,' the policeman said, with a nod to his dad. The policeman's radio was squawking something. He turned and left in a hurry.

Marcus waited for his dad's tirade. There was none. Instead, there were tears in his dad's eyes as he spoke. 'Marcus?'

'Y ... yes?' Marcus stammered. Seconds later Marcus felt his dad's arm's pressing into his back and the musty familiar smell of his old jumper comforted him. His dad pinched his cheeks, 'so you went for a little walk, did you?' he said.

'Yeh,' said Marcus into his dad's jumper.

'Sometimes we need ... be alone. I took walks alone at your age,' Dad said.

'Don't encourage him,' said his mum, who was now in the room as well, scowling. 'Is anyone hungry?' she said softly. Leah was sleeping in his mum's arms.

'Me,' said Marcus. Automatically, he stretched out his arms. His mum placed Leah in them and went into the kitchen.

It was bizarre. Moments later, even though it was the middle of the night, they were all sat at a table eating pancakes. For a minute there was silence. Then his mum blurted out, 'How could you do this, Marcus? How could you? Where have you been?'

Marcus told them the truth, that he had been to Adele's and then down to the river, and he had thought about jumping in.

'You scare me, Marcus,' said his mum. 'What about Leah? You're her brother. You can't leave Leah.'

'I wouldn't jump in that river,' said Dad. 'You wouldn't drown, but you'd end up sailing along on a used tyre, with raw sewage wrapped round your head.'

Marcus laughed. The first time he'd laughed all day. His dad laughed too. Mum scowled then gave in and laughed with them. They laughed together so much Marcus's cheek muscles went into spasms. He couldn't remember the last time all of them had laughed together like this round the kitchen table. Yet there was sadness casting a shadow on his mum's face that Marcus had never seen before.

KARMA AND SHOPPING VOUCHERS

Next morning it was Saturday. Marcus came down to find his dad wearing an African style robe. Marcus nodded, not sure what to say. Dad was sat on the sofa together with Mum. Mum looked tired. Dad's head hung low, as though the two of them had been talking for a long time.

'Marcus, sit down, we want to talk to you,' said Dad.

The dreaded talk. Marcus sat.

'You know it's difficult for us both, chasing around earning money to pay the bills, a new baby to take care of, but, well, I'm trying to imagine what your Granddad would say, the fella up there on the wall. The chief.'

'And?'

'I think he'd say, "we've got to work together and think about this without emotion and without fear". We love you, but tears won't solve your problems. We have to dry our tears and find out how we can help you.'

'Was granddad really a chief, Dad?'

'They gave him the name as an honour. He was not born a chief, he became one.' Dad turned back to Marcus's mum. 'I think the Big Guy on the wall up there wants me to spend more time with his grandson. Quality time.' He turned to Marcus. 'What do you say, Marcus?'

'Sure,' Marcus said. It was true he never really saw his dad, let alone hung out with him.

'Maybe me and Marcus can go shopping together?' Dad said to Mum.

Marcus groaned. He hated shopping. How was that quality time? His parents had plotted this.

'Deal!' said Mum quickly. She rummaged in her handbag. 'And here's the vouchers to get discounts off the prices.'

Marcus groaned again. Vouchers. He'd be a laughing stock if anyone saw him at the checkout, next to his dad fumbling around with shopping coupons.

'Great,' said Dad. 'And let's get some oil for his skin, it looks dry. And some gel for his hair. Add those to the list–'

'Dad! No gel!' If there had been a big hole in the living room, Marcus would gladly have fallen into it.

Fifteen minutes later, Marcus was sat next to his dad on the free Saturday bus service from the estate to ASDA. He had his ATC under his foot. He had his hearing aids in because Dad insisted. And he had his upper lip curled high in distaste so everyone could see he hated shopping. Dad was going through Mum's two-page printed out shopping list like there was some hidden code in it. This was so uncool. Marcus sighed loudly, but Dad didn't seem to notice.

Then a miracle happened. When they reached ASDA, Dad went through the supermarket aisles grabbing things quick as a fox. In fifty swipes of the self-serve scanner they were in and out. It took them under twenty minutes. He didn't even use the coupons.

'How did you know where everything was?' Marcus asked afterwards, astonished. They were back outside, with four bags of shopping each.

'Shopping is war,' Dad said. 'The supermarkets try to keep you in there as long as possible, and my battle plan is to get out as fast as I can. And today, I won!' Dad laughed.

They reached the bus stop for the free bus back to the estate. Marcus decked his ATC. His toes tingled. He wanted to practice.

'Go on then, show me what you can do,' Dad said.

'I'm not in the mood.'

A green haired goth passed by, pushing a trolley. Dad got to his feet. 'What do you mean, "not in the mood?" Pass me the ball, I'll show you some tings!'

Reluctantly, Marcus rolled the ball to his dad's feet. He wondered how fast an ambulance could arrive at the supermarket car park if his dad tripped over and broke a leg.

Dad stabbed at the ball. It rose up at an angle. He chased it and kicked it higher, then juggled it a little bit clumsily up to his right knee twice. Then let it fall to the ground.

'Not bad, Dad, you're improving,' Marcus said, generously. He listened to the ball, noticing how the bounce on the tarmac sounded sharper and longer with his hearing aids in. He could also hear his dad's keys jangling in his pocket when he kicked the ball.

'Bet you can't do better!' his dad called out to him.

Grinning, Marcus went through his full repertoire. He saw his dad's face go from appreciation to respect, to amazement. A bunch of shoppers stopped to watch him, but it was only his dad that Marcus really noticed.

'Again,' his dad was saying, 'higher! Yes! That's my son! Now give it me!'

Marcus knocked the ball over to his dad. Dad did a few wonky keepy-uppys that had the crowd picking up their shopping and moving on, then knocked the ball back to Marcus.

Marcus did his Cryuff Turn, his Marseille Roulette then booted the ball forty metres high. He waited, waited, waited. He heard it whistling through the air as it zeroed down. He took two small steps to his left then killed the ball dead under his left foot. The crowd clapped. Dad patted him on the shoulder. 'This is my boy,' he said, 'I raised him. This is my boy!'

They got home and unpacked. Nobody else was in. When the stuff was all finally in the cupboards, his dad said: 'Time for our reward, don't you think?' He swung open the fridge door. The reward was a glass of fresh orange each.

'Do you think God is punishing me by making me deaf, Dad?' Marcus asked once he'd gulped down the orange juice. 'Have you heard of karma?'

'Steady on, steady on, what are you talking about?'

'"Do good things and good things happen to you. Do bad things and bad things happen to you". Buddhism. I found it on the Internet. Is that why my ears don't work, because I've done bad things?'

Dad shook his head. 'I don't know about Buddhism, but it's no one's fault. Things simply happen. You know the saying, "stuff happens"? That's how life is. Stuff happens. We learn to deal with it, and that's what forms our character, makes us stronger. Motorway crashes. Floods. Accidental tape deletes. Nobody deserves these things. They just happen. Somehow we cope.'

'I don't know if I can cope,' Marcus said quietly.

'Come here.' Marcus's dad wrapped him in his arms. 'You only need the strength for one day, Marcus, not every day that you can see coming at you. Live in the now. Think of things you can enjoy now and find contentment in those.'

'Is that African philosophy, Dad?' Marcus said, breaking away from his embrace.

'It's your granddad's philosophy. What's the worst that can happen to you?'

'I could go completely deaf.'

'Okay. What sounds annoy you?'

Marcus had a think. 'Whiny motorbikes,' he said. 'Being yelled at to wake up and get to school. The debt collector's *knock knock knock knock*.'

'All that you'd be free of,' Dad said.

'Yeah, the bright side. People keep telling me about it.'

'C'mon. From what the doctors say, you are not about to go completely deaf, so put that out of your mind. One day at a time, Marcus,' Dad said, squeezing his shoulder. 'Okay?'

They were sitting on the sofa in the living room now. His dad's yellowing eyes were steady, kind and a bit mashed up. He was starting to look a bit like Granddad.

'Thanks, Dad. I'm going training now,' Marcus said.

'Right,' his Dad said. 'And remember. All that talent in your toes, it all came from me. You tell everyone, you got it from your dad!'

Marcus laughed and dashed out of the house to the pitch.

ALL FOR ONE AND ONE FOR ALL

He was not long at the pitch when Horse showed up. Marcus flicked his ATC to him. Horse stabbed it up, headed it twice then rolled it back to him. Marcus trapped the ball, flipped it up, caught it in the crook of his neck, rolled it over the crown of his head and nestled it on his forehead a second. He let it fall slowly forwards, popped it with his right knee then booted it high in the air. The ball soared away on a perfect ninety degree angle, stopped on the third second, zoomed down, and on the sixth second was suddenly right there by them. Marcus effortlessly cushioned it with his left knee and trapped it under his left foot.

'Not bad,' said Horse, momentarily in awe, then, 'what a show off you are, Marky!'

Marcus smiled. It was true.

They switched to tackling each other. Horse was the better tackler. Marcus marvelled at the swish, click and crunch sounds Horse's feet made as he scrabbled on the tarmac. By the fifth winning tackle, Horse's pride was redeemed. They stopped and sat on the low wall bordering the pitch for no reason other than the sun was in their faces and it felt good. He heard cars zoom by behind him. He'd never heard them rattle like they were today. It was because of the pot holes, he decided.

'We've missed you,' Horse said.

Marcus shrugged. 'Water under the bridge.'

'The school's stupid. They're punishing the whole team. It's unfair. And what for? Deciding you've taken enough stick from Miss Podborsky? I'd have done the same. Stuff her! Stuff the school! Stuff everything!' Horse jumped off the wall in his excitement.

Marcus couldn't have put it better himself.

'We need you back in the team.'

'You could still win the final,' Marcus said.

Horse scowled. 'It's all down to the players, right? I'm not dissing Leonard, but he's not you. Whatever the coach says, he's the chorus line, not the ballerina.'

'What are you talking about?' said Marcus dreamily. The sun was on his face and he closed his eyes. His mind drifted to the hearing test in the gloomy grey booth, and he shivered, remembering it.

Horse poked him on his shoulder. Marcus opened his eyes again.

'You saw it in training. When we need the bullets, when we need the fat lady to come on and sing, close the ballet down, that's you, not Leonard. You can't have three takes to do something in a real match. It's got to be – bang – first time.'

'I'm the fat lady?'

'Yeh.'

'The ballerina?'

'Yeh.'

'The *fat* ballerina?'

They laughed.

'You know what I mean. What I'm saying is —'

'I get you,' said Marcus. 'But Leonard's okay. He does a job.'

'Yeh, well "okay" won't be good enough.'

Marcus went back to practising left-right switches. Horse was suddenly busy on his phone.

Marcus tried flip-turn-pass, first left foot, then right. He noticed when he did the move on the tarmac, it made an exact pattern of sounds. He was about to move on to drag-backs when he spotted Jamil walking up, swinging his kit bag. Then Ira arrived, together with Leonard, both also in their football kit. The three of them ran over to him, Ira and Jamil grinning ear to ear.

'What's going on?' Marcus called out to Horse. It had to be Horse.

Horse fessed up. 'I rang them. Team meeting!'

Everyone sat on the wall. Horse stood directly in front of Marcus and explained it all. 'You've got to come back to school, Marcus, we need you. Training is rubbish without you.'

'And there's no way we're ever going to win that final without your skills,' chipped in Ira.

'You add something,' said Leonard, 'it's true.'

'I don't want to go back,' said Marcus, though the flip of heart he just felt told him otherwise. He'd missed his friends more than anything.

'It's that stuff about your ears, right?' said Horse.

Marcus nodded.

'But that's sorted now, ain't it?' said Ira. 'So come back!' Ira shook his waxy black, shoulder length hair in emphasis. He was a general on the field, like Horse, though Ira was in charge of the defence.

'I don't want to go to school wearing these hearing aids,' Marcus said. He felt stupid even as he said it. But it was what he felt.

'You mean you're wearing them now?' asked Horse.

Marcus nodded again.

'Anybody notice that?' Horse asked.

Everybody shook their heads.

Horse leaned over and looked closely at Marcus. 'Okay, *now* I can just about see them. Just. So what's the big deal? C'mon, Marcus. We need you on the team if we're gonna win this Cup. That means you've got to go to school. That's the start, you know how it works. If you got to wear those to school, then fine. Tell you what, we'll all wear them. Where did you get them? We'll all wear them, right?'

Everyone nodded again. Even Leonard.

Marcus laughed. 'It's not that simple. You can't just get them like that. You've got to be a bit deaf.'

'We can fake it,' said Jamil. 'What? What? What? I beg pardon?' he said, swivelling his head. Everyone laughed. They were laughing with Marcus, not at him this time. He laughed along.

'Look Marky,' said Horse, 'we'll stand with you, man. We need you. C'mon.'

They were all around him now, tugging at him, pleading.

'What do you say?' said Horse. 'Do it for us.' Horse started messing with his hair. It always got to him, that, it was like being tickled, and Horse knew it.

'Alright, alright,' Marcus said, fending Horse off his hair and finally relenting.

'Yes!' whooped Jamil. He did his crazy jig across the pitch. Everyone else broke out into high-fives and hugs.

Nobody seemed to care that although he was agreeing to go back to school, he was still banned from the team. But what did he know? Marcus thought. Maybe they were right. Maybe there was a way back into the team.

'Let's train then,' said Marcus. 'We're gonna have to be sharp to win!'

They practiced tackling. Leonard and Marcus played on the same side and won all three rounds. They high-fived at the end of it, the first time the two of them had ever done that. Marcus liked the crisp, deep, *smack* sound their high-five made, when their hands closed together perfectly. It was a weird feeling for Marcus, working with Leonard, but good. They did heading exercises and some other stuff, all organised by Leonard. They only stopped when the light faded so badly they were running into one another. Dragging his tired legs home, Marcus thought, sometimes, try as hard as you did, you couldn't escape your friends. And even though you didn't know it at the time, sometimes you needed them.

THE SEAS PART

Next morning, Marcus told his mum he was prepared to go back to school. His mum blushed with excitement and cooked him rice pudding even though he never ate rice pudding for breakfast and didn't want it.

'There is more good news,' his dad said, slurping coffee. 'We wrote to the history teacher, whatsherface about the football. I told her I'm not letting her stop my hugely talented, amazingly gifted son lose his biggest chance in life over some snot-nosed teacher's idea of please and thank you's.'

'Geography teacher,' Marcus corrected him.

'Same difference,' said Dad.

For once Marcus was impressed. His dad never wrote down anything but lyrics. 'You wrote the school an email? I'm surprised you didn't sing it down the phone, Dad.'

'Something like that,' said Dad.

'Nothing like that,' said Mum. 'I wrote the email. And I phoned her too.'

'But we talked about it together,' said Dad. 'I advised. And the school will un-ban you from the football team or my name's not Johnny Kudos,' Dad declared. 'All you've got to do is turn up.'

'Your name *isn't* Johnny Kudos. Your *real* name's not Johnny Kudos,' Mum said.

Marcus could see they were about to get into it again. 'I thought this was about me?' he said.

'It *is* about you, son. Your mother got distracted.'

'I spoke to the Head, and she's personally guaranteed that if you go back, they will un-ban you,' Mum said, 'And I'll go into school with you if you want, and sort this troublesome geography teacher out.'

'No, Mum, please don't.' A clash between Miss Podborsky and his mum would be a supernova event, creating a million light years of embarrassment for him.

'Just say the word,' his mum said, fired up still.

That night, Marcus was scared, but happy. He texted Adele.

The seas part – am bk to skul – skul agreed.

Amazeballs. Hows yr ears

Still on side ov head.

Seriously … (Gud u can joke abt it now)

Fine. Get hedaches sumtimes – 2 much noise

Me 2. Mainly ma n da arguing

Snap

Lols

Xx

Xxxxx

Marcus didn't know how to reply to Adele's last text. It was a kiss race. He sent her a pic of a dog with hearts spinning around it instead.

BACK TO SCHOOL, BACK TO REALITY

In form class, Marcus sat with Jamil in his old seat at the back of the class. Everyone was chatting away. Marcus loved the noisy depth of conversations he now heard, from all round the room, but he found it confusing sometimes, sorting out from which direction voices were coming. Nobody yet seemed to have noticed his hearing aids. He messed with his phone, going through messages and trying at the same time to get used to how loudly the chairs scraped the floor in the classroom. Then his form teacher was suddenly on his shoulder. He was reading a text Adele had sent him the morning after he had run off from her place. The teacher saw it and before he could hide the phone, read it out loud enough for Jamil to hear.

"'*U r my morning sunshine. Thanks 4 last nites kiss.*' Very sweet. I wish someone was my morning sunshine!'

Marcus blushed. Jamil guffawed and poked Marcus in the ribs with his pen.

At the front of the class, the teacher started explaining the new rules about dining room times. Someone interrupted her. 'Excuse me, Miss, can you say that again for thicko Marcus back there, please?'

It was Evan.

'He may not have heard you,' Evan continued, 'have you got your hearing aids switched on, Marcus, eh, eh, eh?'

There were sniggers. The whole class turned to look at Marcus.

Marcus could feel his tear ducts swelling. Everyone in class was watching him. He thought of his dad's words. 'Don't let them rile you.'

'I can hear Miss fine,' Marcus replied to Evan, nonchalantly, 'and thanks for the "thicko" compliment, Evan. From someone who gets D's in everything, that really means something!'

The whole class erupted, but this time laughing at Evan. The form teacher let it settle then resumed her drone about new dining room rules.

In the corridor after form class, Jamil tripped over a school-bag and accidentally punched Evan in the face as he fell. That was Jamil's story and he was sticking to it. Everyone in the class who had seen it backed Jamil up. Marcus told Jamil he didn't need protecting from Evan's cowardly mouth. Still, Marcus liked what Jamil had done. Evan deserved it. He would have done it himself only he was trying to stay un-banned so he could play in the final. After all the effort he'd made, nothing was going to get in his way on that.

The next lesson was maths. It was then that Jamil told Marcus his eye had been hurting him ever since he got punched in the last game and sometimes he couldn't see the writing on his textbook because the page started swimming away. Marcus told Jamil he had to get to the doctors fast, but by the end of maths, Jamil was saying he was okay again.

The coach welcomed him with wind-milling arms at training that afternoon. 'Marky, we've missed you massive!' He took him to one side. 'I know you've had problems with your ears,' he said. 'But the problem's with your ears, right, not your feet. I know you can't wear your hearing aids for the football and I've worked something out. We're going to practice it today. When the ref blows his whistle tomorrow, in the final – you've not forgotten it's the final, right? When the whistle blows, everyone's gonna raise their hands, so you know the whistle's gone, okay? We've practised it, everyone knows. Get it?'

'Yeh,' said Marcus. 'And thanks, Mr Davies.'

'Don't be soft, lad. Now you're back, we've got one hand on the Cup already. I'm working on my victory speech for next assembly!'

Marcus laughed. Even Mr Davies knew he did bad assembly speeches. They walked over together to the football pitch. 'Alright, boys, box work, let's go,' said the coach. 'Accuracy. Show them, Marcus.' They did box-to-box pass exercises, twists and turns and throw-in drills. Then Mr Davies called them all together. 'Defence, midfield, tomorrow don't give Bowker the space to play. Press up and attack the ball. Got it? Let's practice that. Leonard set the cones up.'

Leonard was playing tomorrow in place of Rocket who had the flu. The coach said it would make the midfield more solid anyway. Given a choice, Marcus would have opted for Rocket in the team, but there was no choice.

They worked till the defence got the hang of how to force play further and further up the field. Then the light faded to nothing. The coach blew his whistle.

Automatically everyone put their hand up. Marcus smiled. He'd heard the whistle that time anyway, but it still helped.

'Right lads … last run.'

Everyone groaned.

'Get on with it!' Mr Davies yelled. 'No pain, no gain! It's … quick and the dead! When the going gets tough …'

Groaning even more at the coach's clichés, everyone did one last sprint up and down the dark field.

In the dressing room, Horse approached Mr Davies. 'Have you read this, Sir?' he asked. It was an article from the Bowker Vale website that Horse had printed out. Everyone knew about it. Mr Davies looked it over then read it aloud to them all:

A Battle Royale looks set to take place this Tuesday with Bowker Vale challenging Ducie for the Schools League Cup. It's a game that Bowker Vale are convinced they will win. Bowker Vale have swept all before them this year. Their temporary coach, the Level 2 FA Coach Qualified, Mr Vialli said: "Winning on Saturday will be a high probability. Bowker Vale is a science academy and we take a scientific approach. Our boys get the correct nutrition, the correct preparation, and the correct drill. No disrespect to our opponents, Ducie, their hearts are in the right place, but I don't see them troubling us. Some say Ducie are weak. Others say they are a one player team. Yet whatever team they put out on that pitch, we are confident of victory.

With rumours of a Manchester United scout taking a serious interest in the School League Final, and ready to offer an apprenticeship to the best player of the game, this may yet prove to be the match of the season in the school boy football world."

There was silence.

'There you go, lads,' Mr Davies said, '"A weak, one player team". That's what they think of you.' He screwed the article up and kicked it into the showers. 'Tomorrow's chip paper. Don't be fooled. It's just mind games. We'll do our talking on the pitch tomorrow! Right? I can't hear you. Right?'

'Yeeaaaaah! Yeeaaaaah!' Everyone left the changing room with their tonsils sore from yelling, 'YEAH!'

That evening, when he got home, Marcus rushed upstairs and plugged in his phone to recharge it. In twelve hours' time he would be playing in the Cup final. Maybe he would even become the Manchester United apprentice. He imagined rubbing shoulders with Wayne Rooney in the Man United dressing room, Ryan Giggs wandering by and showing him a better way to tie his boots, maybe a friendly pat on the shoulder from Rio Ferdinand. He dreamed about playing five-a-side with them in quick passing games. His charger light changed from red to blue. Marcus switched the phone on. He saw a text from Dwayne, the Bowker Vale striker:

We doin it bro

Marcus guessed Dwayne meant they were going to take on Mr Vialli, though he didn't know quite how. Whatever they had planned, Mr Vialli deserved it. End of, as Horse loved to say. Marcus texted Adele.

U ok w yr Pops?

She texted him back straight away:

Had a heart to heart w mum & she told dad off. But he aint neva gonna change. Big game 2moro?

Yeh. U gona b deh?
Of Cz. N I wnt u 2 win. Dwn wth rcsts!
Thnx. Gna get sleep now
Bye xxx
Bye xxx

It was the x's at the end of Adele's last text that put the smile on Marcus's face. Kisses. It was mad stupid, but they spun his head. He could hear voices downstairs. He realised he still had his hearing aids in. He listened. It was his parents, rowing again. Marcus switched off his hearing aids and put them away. That was one advantage, he thought. He didn't have to listen if he didn't want to. He wasn't interested in his parents' rows, he needed to concentrate on the match, visualise how he was going to play, re-run all the moves he'd practised.

THE CUP FINAL

School dragged, but classes eventually ended. The team met at the school gates. They were taking a taxi-van to Bowker Vale. Marcus began kicking his ATC around as they waited for the final players to show up. Half an hour later, with the driver getting impatient, Mr Davies let them all on board. Andrew skidded into the bus and scrambled on board.

'Right, seatbelts, lads!' Mr Davies began a head count.

Jamil still wasn't here yet. Marcus texted Jamil, telling him he needed to get here fast, they were about to leave. As Mr Davies passed him on his head count, he handed Marcus a folded up note. Marcus read it. 'Good luck with the Cup Final.' Signed 'Miss Podborsky'. Marcus didn't know what to make of it. He shoved the note inside his bag.

The driver started the engine. 'Sir, where's Jamil?' shouted Horse above the din.

'Yeh, he's not here!' everyone joined in.

'Bad news,' said the coach, 'just got a text. After training last night, Jamil felt really bad with his eye. Long story short, the hospital says he's got a hairline fracture of his eye socket and can't play. But Kwong's here. You're playing, Kwong!'

Kwong smiled, but everyone went quiet. Kwong had only just joined the school, and he hadn't really shown them anything special in training, at least nothing that Marcus had seen.

'Come on, pick your heads up,' said the coach, 'this is your big day, we're gonna win. Right? Away we go, driver!'

The van rumbled on for half an hour. The mood soon picked up and everyone talked over one another. The match had been rearranged to Bowker Vale after the turf controversy at Ducie, Marcus learned.

The van sounded like it had a hundred more moving parts than he'd imagined before, as though there were a hundred elves all under the bus floor, tapping away. It was a diesel engine. He'd learned how to tell the difference with engines. Diesels were noisier. Some of the team already had their football boots on and he listened to the different sounds the different studs made on the van floor – how plastic studs sounded different to metal ones. He heard Kwong's voice, all excited now he was playing. Kwong sounded like he came from London. He hardly knew him, but he already liked Kwong. His hands were always drumming on surfaces and Kwong pressed his lips together whenever he didn't like what you were saying and he covered his mouth when he laughed. His skin was the colour of mayonnaise, except his knees which were black with scabs. He was brave. He'd never seen Kwong shrink from a big tackle or pull out of a diving header.

Finally, they arrived at Bowker Vale school. They drove up a long, private road lined with trees. They got out of the van. Bowker was a combination of old grammar school building and smart new extension. Everything was spotless and shiny. They were shown to swanky changing rooms that were kitted out with power showers, under-floor heating and automatic boot cleaning machines. You stuck your shoes in the machine while still wearing them and it cleaned the muck off them. Everyone was quiet, hesitating even to put their kit bags on the glossy wooden benches.

'Don't be impressed lads,' said the coach, 'It's just money.' He waved a derisory hand at the decor. 'Shallow stuff. You can dress a chicken up in wolf's clothing, it's still a chicken, right?' The coach then farted. Marcus had never heard a fart so loud and extended.

Everyone groaned and laughed, but it was like his fart broke a spell and the usual noise went up as they got changed. Nobody had seen the referee. Normally he popped his head into the changing rooms, introduced himself, checked studs and shook hands with the coach. It wasn't compulsory, but it was the way things were usually done.

Horse led them out onto the pitch. Bowker were not yet out. Marcus looked around. There were at least a hundred people on the side-lines of the pitch. He spotted Mr Vialli, standing with Adele. There was a big group of adults around Mr Vialli as well, the parents of Bowker Vale players, Marcus guessed. The Man United scout was among them. Adele waved to Marcus. Marcus nodded to her then did some hip-twist exercises. 'Concentration'. The coach had given him a Post-It note in the taxi-van with that one word written on it.

On the far side of the pitch there were more people waving at Marcus. He looked carefully. There was some old man with a dog. Nero!

Nero's ears pricked high and his tail was wagging like a helicopter blade. He began tugging at his lead.

'Sit!' Marcus called out to him. Even from the distance, Marcus saw Nero sit.

And who was that? It couldn't be. His dad! Waving and shouting his name. Marcus waved back, amazed. He'd never played in front of his dad before. It was going to be weird, but a good weird. A man in a suit and tie strode out with a microphone in his hand and stood in the centre of the pitch.

A crackly sound echoed around. 'Can we … lights?'

Marcus looked around. The sound was coming out of some speakers attached high up on a set of pillars. Floodlights. Bowker had floodlights! Marcus's eyes boggled. As he watched, the floodlight bulbs jerked on. Suddenly Marcus had four shadows. He carried on doing his warm-up exercises, all five of him, as the Bowker Head talked on into the microphone, not ten metres away:

'Ladies and gentlemen, welcome to Bowker Vale, I'm Doctor Bentley the headteacher here. The winner of the match will win the All Schools Trophy. Thank you all for coming and supporting this occasion. Let's have a great game!'

The Bowker Head walked off. There was then a fanfare through the speakers and the Bowker Vale team ran onto the pitch. They formed two lines and did two-footed hops, interweaving with each other at precise intervals, left then right, then left then right. They span around and did the same thing again, right then left, right then left.

Mr Davies was running around on the Ducie side of the pitch in his sleeping-bag-coat, yelling. 'Pay no attention, lads, this isn't a synchronised swimming contest, it's a football match!'

Marcus turned his back on the Bowker Vale warm-up. He got hold of the match ball and began juggling it. It was an ATC. Marcus smiled. His favourite ball. He smacked the ball over to Horse and it dropped exactly at Horse's feet a hundred metres away.

The pitch was smooth and had an artificial green sheen to it. It reminded him of the ASDA goth's green head, only flat. Around them was a motorway flyover, a field with two horses, then more fields. Through thickening clouds, Marcus could just make out a pyramid-shaped, blue glass building in the distance. He wondered what it was.

'Marcus, the game, yeh? Concentrate!' yelled the coach.

Back on the pitch, Marcus could see Horse pointing at something. It was the referee, trotting out. The same black referee as they'd had in the league decider! Horse jogged over to him with Mr Davies, as did Anthony Vialli and Anthony's dad. A photographer ran up and had the two captains pose with the referee. The referee tossed the coin. Bowker won the toss and kept their end. Then something weird happened.

Instead of taking their places, Dwayne, Little Mo and four other Bowker Vale players turned and walked off the pitch. They stood in a row on the Bowker touchline, arms crossed, faces defiant.

In the floodlights, it seemed like there were thirty of them, not six.

The referee was puzzled. He put his whistle to his mouth again. Mr Vialli went over to them and began shouting. Marcus drifted over, as did Horse, Andrew and Kwong.

'Forget it. I've told you, lads. Simple. I don't do apologies!' Mr Vialli was shouting at them.

'Then we're not playing,' Dwayne replied calmly.

Anthony was standing next to his dad. 'Are you an idiot?' he said to Dwayne. He shoved him, trying to loosen his crossed arms. Dwayne resisted. He grabbed Dwayne by the waist, trying to drag him onto the pitch. Dwayne pushed him off.

Anthony turned around and spotted Marcus. 'This is all your doing, isn't it?' he accused him. 'I hope … happy now!'

Marcus shrugged. 'I didn't say the "B" word. Your dad did.'

Mr Davies had come over. 'Come on, lads, be reasonable,' he said to the Bowker players, 'it's a football match, not auditions for Joan of Arc. Let's get going, those floodlights must cost the earth to keep on.' Mr Davies's words had no effect.

Adele had run over. Marcus watched her, wondering what she was going to do. She lined up with the six and crossed her arms too, facing Anthony, facing her dad, defiant. She looked at Marcus as if to say, 'still think I'm a spy?'

'This is getting silly,' said Mr Vialli, 'I give in. I'm sorry. I shouldn't have said what I said.'

'And?' said Dwayne.

'This is my last match in charge. The proper coach's chemotherapy treatment is going well. He'll soon be back. There. I've promised,' he said. 'Now let's play … I'm sorry. Please?'

Dwayne looked to Little Mo. Little Mo nodded.

There was a cheer from all round as the Bowker Vale Six ran back onto the pitch. As they did so, Dwayne knocked fists, momentarily, with Marcus.

'That was cool, bro,' Marcus said to Dwayne.

'Yeh. And now we're … to thrash you,' said Dwayne, 'that's gonna be even cooler!'

'Game on!' Marcus replied, grinning.

At kick-off Bowker quickly won the ball and got their well grooved pass-and-move game going. Marcus and the Ducie midfield chased shadows. It was as if they were playing on a bar football table, but with the Bowker end lifted up so that the ball always rolled towards the Ducie goal, no matter what Ducie did.

After two Bowker corners, the ball finally fell to Marcus. He squared it to Leonard, who shunted it up for Kwong to chase on the wing. Kwong trapped it and went on a mazy run straight into four defenders, who tussled the ball back off him. The Bowker pinball machine moved back into overdrive.

Mr Davies tried to rally them: 'Tuck in. Leonard! Kwong push up! Horse, tighter! Marcus, into space! Ira … there! Press!'

Horse slid into a tackle and came out with the ball at his feet. But his hand went up. Marcus looked. The whistle had blown. Meanwhile the boy he'd tackled, Anthony, was rolling on the floor, all four limbs jerking like he'd just showered in itching powder.

The referee reached for his cards. Horse groaned. 'Referee!' he protested, 'Look! I won the ball!'

Ira pushed him away from the ref. The ref took a yellow card out of his pocket. But he didn't move towards Horse. Instead, he turned, waited for Anthony Vialli to stop rolling, then showed the card to Anthony.

There was pandemonium on the Bowker Vale touchline. Mr Vialli jumped up and down on the spot, jabbing away: 'Referee! What was that? Call yourself a referee? You stupid, blind, b…'

The referee looked straight over at Mr Vialli. His hand hovered by his chest pocket.

Mr Vialli's protest fizzled out. 'Er good call, whatever!' Mr Vialli said, turning away.

The referee nodded to Mr Vialli. His hand slowly lowered from his pocket.

Marcus took the free kick. He floated it high over the Bowker goal area, seeking out Horse. Horse stumbled and fell, but Kwong leaped and connected with a thumping header. The ball whacked the crossbar and came out. Leonard trapped it and thundered in a shot. A Bowker defender stuck out an arm to stop the ball. The ball cannoned off the outstretched arm. Ducie appealed as one. 'Penalty!'

The referee gave it straight away. There was no dissent from Bowker this time.

Leonard had the ball at his feet. He looked across at Marcus. Mr Davies was waving and yelling. He beckoned them both over. 'Marcus, take it. I want it drilled high to the goalkeeper's left. Your right, the goalkeeper's left. Got it? I've done the research. That's an order. Now go!'

Over at the penalty spot mark, the referee was tapping his watch, his hand getting itchy around his pocket again.

Marcus rested the ball against his head as he eyed the goal.

'Referee! Excessive hair grease!'

Even Marcus heard Mr Vialli's bellow, his latest ludicrous protest.

'It's oil, not grease,' Marcus said to the referee at his shoulder.

The referee flicked the ball up from the spot with his left foot, wiped it on his shirt then dropped it down on the spot again. 'Carry on,' he said to Marcus with a sigh.

Marcus eyed the keeper then looked to the ref. The ref nodded to him that he could take the kick. Marcus took six slow steps back then ran up. He drilled it exactly where the coach said. The ball shot off his foot and was billowing in the back of the Bowker net before the goalkeeper had even moved.

Next he knew, his dad was kissing him and singing, 'Mighty goal! Mighty goal! What a mighty goal!'

'Dad, get off the pitch. Now!' Marcus said, grinning and jogging his way back to the halfway line in a mob of Ducie players, plus his dad.

At the restart, Bowker poured players forward. Ducie defended desperately. There was a goalmouth scramble and a Bowker defender poked the ball into the Ducie net. 1–1.

'Come on, lads, heads up!' rallied Mr Davies but the Bowker onslaught happened again. They pinged the ball at dizzying speed across the Ducie half and into the penalty area. The ball sped to Anthony. Anthony poised to meet it on the volley. It looked a certain goal. From nowhere, Leonard threw himself head first at the ball. He got there just in time. The ball bounced off his head. Anthony's foot smashed into Leonard's face.

It looked bad.

The St John's Ambulance crew ran onto the pitch.

Mr Davies stood over Leonard, dribbling water over his head. 'Get up, Lenny, come on, get up, you're a hero, now get up for God's sake, we've got no subs!' The St John's crew sat Leonard up and bunged his nose with cotton wool. The bleeding stopped. Leonard got groggily to his feet. The referee inspected the paramedic's handiwork. He was satisfied, just, and let Leonard stay on the pitch.

Bowker Vale took their corner. Someone headed it. There was a goalmouth scramble. The ball squirted to Horse and he hoofed it up to the Bowker penalty area. Kwong was lurking there. He span off his marker, slipped around the final defender and shot. A classy side foot bang into the back of the net. 2–1. Kwong fell to the floor, arms raised. Marcus dived on top of him followed by Ira, then Leonard.

'Alright! Alright!' The referee broke it up.

Bowker kept possession for the last twenty minutes, but Ducie managed to keep them at bay. At half-time the score was still 2–1.

Marcus ran off to the Ducie touchline with the rest of the Ducie players. They had been the underdogs, yet here they were 2–1 ahead. The coach wasn't so impressed. He waved away all the parents then ripped into the team.

'Midfield, you're going off like popcorn in a microwave. Every direction! Pop! Pop! Pop! Think! Defence, get organised! Close them down! It's the emperor's clothes, lads. Don't be so mesmerised. Get stuck in. This can go either way. Concentrate!'

As he was blasting them, Mr Davies handed them orange slices and chocolates. He then knelt down by Marcus.

'Nice penalty, Marcus, but step it up now, okay? Leonard's weakening and our defence can't hold out forever. Show them what you're made of, yeah? You're a star, now's the time to shine, understand? Get your chest out and your head up. Run the show!'

'Got you,' said Marcus. Mr Davies was right. It was time to show them all what he could do, he thought.

Suddenly, Jamil appeared out of nowhere. 'Sir! Sir!' he shouted. He was booted up and had his kit on. 'Sir! I can play. I'm ready. Put me on, Sir!'

The coach looked at him with squinted eyes. Jamil had a Phantom of the Opera mask on. 'No way, Jamil. No!' said Mr Davies flatly.

'The doctor says I can play so long as I wear this mask! Please, Sir!'

'No,' the coach repeated.

'But this is discrimination against one-eyed people!' Jamil pleaded, to peals of laughter. He dropped to his knees and put his hands together. 'Please, Sir, please! I've got a doctor's note giving me permission.'

'Give it here,' the coach said, softening. He snatched the piece of paper Jamil had fished out of his shorts and looked at it for a while with pursed lips. Around Marcus a few hands went up. Marcus looked. The referee was blowing to restart the match.

'Okay, you're the substitute,' said Mr Davies finally. 'Stay on the touchline and I'll see if I need to play you.' Then he called Leonard and Marcus close to him. 'Leonard, good lad, keep going. Stick on that Anthony Vialli. He's the hot dog, you're the bun. Wrap yourself around him. Stop him getting any ketchup then get the ball to Marky.'

'What's the ketchup?' asked Leonard.

'The ball, you ninny.'

'Oh,' said Leonard, 'got it.'

'And Marky, time to take off, right?'

'Got it,' said Marcus.

When the game restarted, Bowker passed the ball neatly and kept possession. It took a while, but finally, Leonard intercepted a stray pass. He booted it up to Marcus. Marcus was stood in the centre circle. As the ATC hit his boot, his dad's song *I Who Have Nothing* started up in his mind. He flipped the ball high, and

194

span round his marker. He swerved past two Bowker midfielders like they were training cones. Over on the right wing, Kwong was calling for the ball. Marcus drilled it sixty yards across to him. It landed perfectly at Kwong's feet. Marcus dashed up the pitch. Kwong swung the ball back high across the penalty area. Marcus flew at it. *All those lonely nights training. All that running. All the hours in the alleyway practising. It was all for this.* The ball dipped and met his right thigh as he jumped. He caught it on his thigh, cushioned it so it fell will him then volleyed the ball straight into the top right corner of the Bowker Vale net. He threw his hands up in joy. Perfect. The Ducie team went wild around him. 3–1. All Marcus could hear was Sylvester's, *I Who Have Nothing.*

After that goal, Bowker faded. Their passing got sloppy. They didn't chase for the ball as hard. Soon Ducie were running riot. At 5–1 a couple of the Bowker players were doubling up on the grass complaining of stomach pains. The St John's Ambulance team rushed on and looked them over. Horse told Marcus that the St John's crew were saying it was either cramp or food poisoning.

The referee blew for the game to continue but again Bowker players began dropping all over the field. Like dying swans, Horse called it, as the game ground to a halt again.

Mr Vialli wanted the game abandoned and argued with the referee. The referee allowed a ten minute interval while all of the Bowker team rushed to the toilet. It helped them a little, but Bowker Vale never got into the game again. Marcus scored a hat trick and made two assists. Jamil came on as a substitute for the last three minutes in place of Kwong. Ducie ran off 7–1 winners.

Afterwards, Mr Vialli came into their dressing room. He shook hands with Mr Davies then spoke to the Ducie players. 'Sorry about that, boys, you deserved a better game. It was some dodgy homemade power juice our team drank at half-time. We'll have to have a look at … formula again, maybe take out the raw eggs. Never mind. Well played. You were the best team on the day. Congratulations. Marcus? Where's Marcus?'

Marcus stood up.

'Marcus, here's the match ball. Man of the match. Total agreement on that, right, Mr Davies?'

Mr Davies nodded.

'First hat trick in a final in twenty years. You've smashed some big records today, boys. Well done.'

'Show your appreciation, lads!' said Mr Davies, 'a magnanimous speech by the losing coach!'

A few players clapped Mr Vialli politely. There was something phoney in how he spoke, Marcus thought, like he was a politician on election day looking for votes. Anyway, one speech wasn't going to change Marcus's mind about him.

When the changing room door swung shut on Mr Vialli, the Ducie celebrations really began. Mr Davies held Marcus's hand up like he was a champion boxer. 'Man of the match. Well done, Marcus!'

'Marcus! Marcus! Marcus!' Everybody began cheering his name. Cans of pop were squirted over his head. The shout switched to 'Ducie! Ducie! Ducie!' and Marcus joined in.

'Alright lads, show some respect. Let's leave this place tidy,' Mr Davies shouted over them. 'Let's show … we're not social housing riff-raff!'

They did a quick clean up, determined to leave the changing room spotless. Marcus put his hearing aids in. He walked out of the changing room with the others feeling giddy with happiness.

In the car park, Marcus's dad hugged him like he'd never hugged him before. 'Woah! Woah! My son is a star!' he cried. Marcus had to laugh. It was beyond embarrassing. His mum was there too with Leah. Marcus kissed his mum, then Leah. He handed his dad the match ball.

'I'll have it framed!' his dad said.

Marcus thought that might be tricky, but he understood what his dad meant.

Both teams were in the car park now, gathered to hear the Manchester United scout make his decision on the apprenticeship.

'I saw a great game today,' the scout said, addressing them all. 'Leonard, you're the Octopus. Best tackler by far. Kept it simple. Fantastic. Bowker's Anthony. Is he here?' Anthony put his hand up. 'Your distribution is first class. You're the postman for Bowker, every ball delivered a hundred percent till you got ill. Excellent positional play, overall reading of the game second to none, I'll be watching both you and Leonard next year.' The scout paused, found Marcus, who was standing next to him, put an arm on his shoulder. 'But what a player Marcus is, eh, everybody? He's the crazy maker. And Marcus is what sets the teams apart. He's the difference between winning and losing. Well done, lad. Man of the match, and well deserved. He's the one we're going to sign!'

There was a loud cheer, though Marcus saw Mr Vialli chuck some papers on the car park tarmac and walk away, jabbing at his phone.

'But what about me?' someone piped up. It was Jamil, pushing himself through the crowd to stand next to the scout. He tugged the scout's jacket sleeve. 'Those five minutes I was on the pitch, I was a sensation, right?' Jamil said.

Everyone laughed.

'What can I say?' said the scout. 'Jamil is Jamil. The merchandise team needs someone your age to model tracksuits and shirts. You look the part, Jamil, at least when you pop your *Phantom of the Opera* mask off. Kwong, you too, if you're up for it?'

Jamil whooped. 'I'm signed by Manchester United! Jamil is handsome! Jamil is the best. Jamil signed by Manchester United! Mr Handsome! Me! Signed by Manchester United! I'm not doing autographs today, you'll all have to wait! I'm tired! Where's the make-up lady? Where's my entourage? Where's my trailer?'

Everyone laughed, even the Bowker players.

The Ducie taxi-van driver beeped his horn.

On the drive back to the school, everyone partied. Amid it all, a text came through to Marcus's phone. It was Adele:

Wel done. U won. How duz it feel?

Brill. Yr bro ok w dat fud poisnin?

He'll live. (She added a sad face here). *Wanna meetup 2moro?*

Yeh.

Gud xx

Xx

The noise in the van dropped. The coach had called them all to attention.

'Well done, lads. I should have had more faith in you. You taught me something. You might be council estate kids, but you got more fight in you, more guts and more brains than any team I've known. The way you've worked together, well, it brings tears to my eyes.'

There was a spontaneous burst of clapping.

'Enough of that. Thank you. Now listen lads, something very important. As you know, it will be my duty to take an assembly tomorrow after this victory. And I've scribbled a speech down here which I want to test out on you.'

Jamil opened a window and screamed: 'Let me out! Let me out!'

'C'mon, Jamil, help me out. You know I've not been too good at this stuff.' Mr Davies cleared his throat and began reading from a piece of paper in a stagey voice:

'When the dust has settled we can view a shining city on a hill. And this hill is called Victory. And it can also be called The Future. And the footholds to the top of that Hill have been hard work, perseverance, truth, justice, late night training, orange slices and an open heart.

'So what do you think, lads?'

'That'll smash it, Sir!' Jamil said instantly. That did it. Everybody was screaming with laughter, even the van driver. Marcus laughed along with them, and yet he felt, somewhere in the coach's clumsy speech, there was a lot of truth. Marcus saw his future. And it did shine. He looked at the last text message on his phone. It was from Adele. He was seeing her tomorrow.

DON'T MISS
THE OTHER BOOKS
IN THE STRIKER SERIES

Funny, hugely entertaining and heartfelt.

'An innovative, impressive and well crafted narrative that strikes a chord for young and old alike. With its numerous resonances, as to the real concerns young adults have, negotiating the choppy waters of growing up.'
Carol Leeming FRSA

Being Me is the perfect companion to The Silent Striker, a feminine take on the football world, being a teenager and figuring out who you are.

'An excellent book! This read quite a lot like a Jacqueline Wilson book with Pakistani characters.'
Ms Yingling Reads, Teacher / Librarian / Blogger, USA

'Mehmood gives us a sterotype-quashing, timely novel about religion, gender, and families. You're Not Proper sounds a resonant, authentic note that cuts through the monotone voices coming out of YA writing.'
Dr Claire Chambers, Huffington Post

'You're Not Proper is a real insight into communities more often talked about than listened to. Full of heart and a cracking good read as well. Highly recommended!'
Melvin Burgess

'Contemporary and hard-hitting. High on impact and highly engaging.'
Jake Hope, *critic, librarian and coordinator of the Lancashire Children's Book of the Year Award.*

Lightning Source UK Ltd.
Milton Keynes UK
UKOW04f0511170316

270327UK00003B/15/P